7/2812

DISCARD

FURY'S
FIRE

Also by Lisa Papademetriou
Siren's Storm

FURY'S FIRE

Lisa Papademetriou

Alfred A. Knopf
New York

THIS IS A BORZOI BOOK PUBLISHED BY ALFRED A. KNOPF

Visit us on the Web! randomhouse.com/teens

Educators and librarians, for a variety of teaching tools, visit us at RHTeachersLibrarians.com

Library of Congress Cataloging-in-Publication Data
Papademetriou, Lisa.
Fury's fire / Lisa Papademetriou. — 1st ed.
p. cm.
Summary: The sequel to Siren's Storm finds best friends Will and Gretchen still haunted by otherworldly goings-on in their beach town on Long Island.
ISBN 978-0-375-86862-7 (trade) — ISBN 978-0-375-96862-4 (lib. bdg.) —
ISBN 978-0-375-89935-5 (ebook)
[1. Supernatural—Fiction. 2. Seaside resorts—Fiction. 3. Sirens (Mythology)—
Fiction. 4. Love—Fiction. 5. Long Island (N.Y.)—Fiction.] I. Title.
PZ7.P1954Fu 2012
[Fic]—dc23
2012008218

The text of this book is set in 11-point Bookman Light.

Printed in the United States of America
July 2012
10 9 8 7 6 5 4 3 2 1

First Edition

To Nick

Acknowledgments

I wish to offer my heartfelt thanks to Ellen Wittlinger, Liza Ketchum, Nancy Werlin, and Pat Collins for their help and, more important, their example. Jessica Bacal, Nerissa Nields, Katryna Nields, Rebecca Serlin, and Heather Abel are endlessly encouraging and understanding, which is just what every writer needs and deserves. I am grateful to my editor, Michele Burke, for her suggestions and insight, and to my agent, Rosemary Stimola, for her courage and nudging. Loving thanks to my husband for his endless enthusiasm and advice to "have fun" with my writing.

Chapter One

Ice begets ice and flame begets flame;
Those that go down never rise up again.
—Sailors' proverb

An uneasy weight hung on Gretchen's chest as she looked around the dim room. *I was dreaming something—what was it?* Gretchen's mind cast about for a train of thought but clutched at emptiness. She couldn't remember. She knew only that she was glad to be awake.

It was that moment before sunrise when the sky has begun to turn gray and the world is filled with shadows. The room was still, but the yellow curtains near her bureau fluttered slightly, and fear skittered down her spine with quick spider steps. "Who's there?" Gretchen asked.

There was a sound like a sigh, and Gretchen's chest tightened in fear. Something was there. By the window. A dark presence. She could almost make out the shape of a man behind the yellow cloth.

Her voice tightened in her throat; she couldn't scream. Someone was in her room. Gretchen's mind reeled, searching for an answer. It was Kirk. Crazy Kirk Worstler—the sophomore who babbled incoherently about seekriegers and angels—had come to kill her. He had stolen into her room once before, to give her a painting. It was a picture of mermaids, a coded message that only he could decipher. . . .

"Kirk?" she whispered. Her voice sounded loud in the still and silent room.

Gretchen sat up. "Kirk?" she said again. She blinked, and the light shifted. The dimness of the gray lifted, like fog burning away in the sun. Suddenly, everything looked different, and she could see clearly.

There was nothing there.

The curtains sagged, and Gretchen understood her mistake. The folds fell at odd angles, suggesting a human form. But the presence she sensed earlier had disappeared completely.

"Dream cobwebs," Gretchen said aloud. That's what her father, Johnny Ellis, called it when you woke up and still had traces of your nightmares clinging to your mind. She pushed back her covers and swung her legs over the side of her bed, and something tore at her ankle.

Gretchen screamed, jumping backward as her cat, Bananas, tumbled from beneath the bedskirt. The feline rolled onto her back playfully, then sat up and curled her tail around her feet, as if nothing had happened and she had no idea why Gretchen was acting so dramatic.

"Cat—" Gretchen started.

Bananas just looked at her, then nonchalantly began to groom her paw.

"Licking my flesh from your claws?" Gretchen asked, rubbing the scratch on her foot. It wasn't bad, really, but it did itch. As if she was offended by the question, the orange and white cat turned and strutted out the half-open door.

As the striped tail disappeared, Gretchen again glanced toward the window. *It was just a dream,* she told herself.

The light shone through the curtains now, and she could see the shape of the tree beyond the window. There was nothing left of the dark presence . . . nothing but the feeling of dread that still sat in Gretchen's chest.

Gretchen yanked off her nightgown and pulled on a pair of red running shorts. She tugged on her sports bra and then ducked into an ancient T-shirt advertising the Old Mill, a cafe in one of the neighboring towns. When she'd lived in Manhattan, Gretchen used to run along the reservoir in Central Park. It was near her Upper East Side apartment, and Gretchen enjoyed running beside the water . . . and the fact that an enormous chain-link fence surrounded the reservoir. She could see it, but she couldn't fall in. Gretchen didn't like water.

Gretchen had never run much at the summer house. There were no sidewalks along the street by her house, so it wasn't really convenient. But now that she and her father were going to be living here full-time, she would have to find a way. Running was what kept her head clear in the cold months. And even though it was only the end of September, the mornings were already turning chilly.

"What are you doing here?" Gretchen asked as she tramped into the kitchen. Her father was sitting at the Formica table, sipping from a cup of coffee and halfheartedly skimming the *New York Times*.

"I live here, remember?" Johnny said. He smiled at her, but it was a smile like a heavy weight—as if it was an effort to make it happen.

"Don't pretend like you're some kind of early riser." Gretchen reached for a banana. "It's six-thirty."

"Couldn't sleep."

Gretchen frowned. "That's not good."

Johnny shrugged. "It happens." He took another long pull of coffee. "I'll feel better once everything arrives."

He meant the things from their Manhattan apartment. Once Johnny had given up the lease, it had taken only two hours for the building manager to find a new tenant. They had been replaced in true New York City style—immediately and without mercy. "When do the movers get here?" Gretchen asked.

"Tomorrow."

Gretchen nodded. She would feel better once her things had arrived, too. Even though she would miss living in Manhattan, she was ready to close that chapter of her life, to write *The End* above it instead of having the pages go on and on with no clear purpose. *Besides,* she thought, *we need the money.*

When her mother had moved out, she had kept custody of most of the funds. Yvonne was an heiress and knew about investments; Johnny had never been in charge of the finances before. So, for a few years, things went on exactly as they had before: Manhattan private school, expensive rent for the apartment, trips abroad. Then, quite suddenly, Johnny realized that they were out of money. A few bad investments and several years of living beyond their means had left them in terrible debt. As a result, they were abandoning the apartment and living in what Gretchen liked to think of as "the ancestral home"—the old farmhouse her grandfather had bought more than half a century ago, which Johnny had inherited, and which he owned free and clear.

As if he were reading her thoughts about finances, Johnny leaned onto one hip and reached for his wallet. "Listen, I wanted to give you something so you could do some back-to-school shopping. . . ." He riffled through the bills, which were mostly ones, and pulled out a couple of twenties. Wincing, he held them out. "I know it's not much."

Gretchen didn't reach for the cash. "It's okay, Dad, I have a job, remember?"

"You're not keeping that job, are you?"

"Sure. Why not?"

Johnny touched the lotus tattoo on his temple. "It's your senior year, Gretchie. You need to keep your grades up."

"They'll stay up."

"That's the most important thing."

"I know, Dad. But I'm going to need to have a job while I'm in college, right? I might as well get used to it."

Johnny looked like he'd been slapped. "I guess I—"

"I didn't—I didn't mean that in a bad way." Gretchen stumbled over her words. "I just meant—"

Johnny dropped the bills on the table. "No, you're right." He shook his head. "I'm sorry, Gretchen."

She touched his shoulder. "It's okay, Dad."

He put his hand over hers but did not look at her. She gave him a playful poke on the shoulder, but he just sighed. "I never worried about money," he admitted. "I guess I thought musicians weren't supposed to care about it."

Gretchen nodded, but she felt her thoughts clouding. The truth—if she dared tell it to herself—was that she was furious with her father for losing all of their money, for not taking care of things. She didn't want to live on Long Island for her senior year. She didn't want to switch schools. She didn't want to stay near the bay, near the bad memories. . . .

But she also loved her father. And one of the things that she loved about him was that he didn't care about money and things in the way that her mother did. Johnny loved people and he loved experiences. He didn't care about cars or jewelry or the right crowd.

She gave him a quick kiss on his tattoo. "Love you."

He looked up at her with his deep gray eyes. "I love you, too, sugar bunny."

Gretchen laughed and tossed the banana peel into the trash. She waved over her shoulder as she headed out the door, her sneakers crunching the gravel still wet with dew.

Gretchen loped along the patchy grass by the side of the road, starting with an easy trot. She passed the falling-down potato barn, gray in the mist, that marked the point at which the Ellis land ended and the Archer farm began. Her muscles were tight, but each pace warmed her, loosening them. A light breeze swept the clammy air over her skin.

She heard a clatter and rumble behind her. Trucks often used this route as a cut-through to the highway. Gretchen moved to the right slightly and kept running. The engine hummed, picking up speed, and the tires crunched over the asphalt as the truck bore down on her.

Gretchen screeched and slammed her shoulder into a hedgerow as the black truck sped past, spewing dirt and rocks with its oversized tires. A chunk of gravel nicked Gretchen's calf. She cursed and inspected the scratch. She would probably have a bruise later, but it wasn't bad. Her heart hammered in her chest as she looked after the truck, which had already disappeared into the mist. She had thought of getting the license plate thirty seconds too late.

What would I have done, anyway? she wondered. *Called the police? The driver didn't see me in the fog.*

Her legs felt weak as she crossed the street. For a moment she considered going back home. But she didn't want to. Momentum carried her forward, and she gathered speed as she ran across the Archer property. She passed the blooming squash patch, the heavy yellow flowers bowing under the weight of the gathered mist. Here and there, pale orange butternut or fat red kuri squashes peeked out from wide green leaves. The squash patch was a long, slim strip—most of the summer people were gone by the end of

September, and there wasn't much of a market for winter squash. Still, some people bought the ornamental gourds and pumpkins. And there were enough gourmet cooks and local restaurants to make the delicatas and carnival squashes worth the ground they grew in.

Gretchen ran past dormant fields and into the small copse of trees. There was little mist here, although it was dark with shade. Still, Gretchen navigated her way easily. The Archer land was as familiar to her as her own, given that her two best childhood friends, Will and Tim, had grown up here.

Through the trees and out toward the sand. The muscles in her legs strained with the change in terrain as Gretchen ran along the mix of sand and rock. Mist hung over the water, and a single dark boulder jutted up through the blanket of fog like a grasping arm. The early-morning sun struggled to break through the clouds, managing only to send down a few pale bars that disappeared before reaching the earth.

Gretchen ran farther, then stopped to rest on a rock. It had been months since she had run, and— although her body felt good—she wasn't used to it. Part of the mist had burned off, and she could see the dark green water, smooth as glass. There was no evidence of the minnows and crabs that lived there, and Gretchen imagined them still sleeping, dreaming their watery dreams.

She pulled at her shirt, which clung to her body with a mix of sweat and fog, and picked up a small stone. It was gray, with a white line through the cen-

ter, smooth and oval. Tim had taught her how to skip
a rock across the water ages ago, and she held it between thumb and forefinger and skimmed it out over
the water. It bounced once, twice, three times, then
hurled itself forward for the final time and landed with
a plop.

"Tim could do seven," Gretchen murmured, leaning back on her elbows. She pictured handsome
ten-year-old Tim, grinning as his rock danced over
the water. Poor Will. He could only send a rock burst-
ing into the water like a cannonball.

Gretchen watched the rings spreading from the
point of final impact. *Pretty,* Gretchen thought as the
fog rolled back like a slow wave. A pale disk appeared
at the place where Gretchen's rock had pierced the
water. Gretchen cocked her head, watching, as a sudden wind kicked up and a ring formed around the
edge of the disk. It didn't disappear. Instead, as the
wind gusted, it grew darker. The center glowed golden
in the early-morning light.

Like an eye, Gretchen thought. Her body felt cold
suddenly, and she was aware of her damp shirt clinging to her skin.

Mist swirled around the dark ring, twisting upward, spouting an oval wall. It gained volume and
grew, like a pillar, toward the dark cloud above. The
cyclone writhed, and slithered slowly toward her.

Gretchen sat perfectly still, hypnotized by the
waterspout. It moved slowly at first, then more quickly.
Suddenly her mind snapped back to reality, and she
struggled to her feet. She stumbled backward, fell,

the rock tearing into her flesh at the same point where the gravel spewed by the truck had hit her. Her hair blew around her face as the wind shrieked like a screaming ghoul.

The waterspout reached toward her, and for a moment Gretchen thought she saw a woman's face—hideous and terrible—in the writhing core. Gleaming golden eyes glared at her with a look of intense hate as air blasted her hair like a wild, cold breath of some ferocious, devouring animal. Gretchen screamed and tried to struggle away as the waterspout moved toward her. But as it reached the edge of the water, it dissipated into the air as suddenly as it had appeared.

Gretchen froze, staring in disbelief. She was so focused on the emptiness before her that she shrieked when a hand clutched her arm.

"Easy," said a voice.

Gretchen looked up into the face of Bertrand Archer—Will's dad. His brow was wrinkled with concern as his warm brown eyes looked down at her. "They can't do much once they reach land."

"You saw it?" That was a relief. At least she hadn't been hallucinating.

"Waterspouts—not that uncommon around here. Seen 'em a few times."

Mr. Archer let go of her arm, and she realized she was shaking. So did he, apparently, because he caught hold of it again. For a moment he said nothing, just looked at her with eyes that were like Will's in shape, but totally different in expression. Mr. Archer was a tall man who liked to joke and laugh with customers, but he was often awkward—almost severe—with Gretchen. "Strange weather."

Gretchen nodded.

"Maybe it's not a good idea to be out by the water like this. Tell you what—why don't you come on home with me? I'm sure Evelyn's cooked up something for breakfast."

The thought of the Archers' cozy yellow kitchen calmed her. "Yes, thank you."

Mr. Archer gave a curt nod and turned. Gretchen followed him.

But she couldn't help casting a final glance over her shoulder.

The surface of the water was smooth as glass again, hiding the dreams and intent of the creatures that lay beneath.

Chapter Two

"Run!" Will cried, urging Gretchen to her feet.

But when Gretchen turned to face Will, he barely recognized her. Her blue eyes burned red—completely red, with no whites. As Gretchen stalked toward them, the seekrieger holding Will shrieked, released her grip, and raced back into the water.

The seekriegers screeched and wailed. The water churned as they plunged below the surface. Gretchen strode into the water.

"No!" Will shouted. "Don't go to them!" He reached for Gretchen, but she grabbed his hand in a grip that burned. Screaming, he writhed and tried to free himself from her grasp. But when he turned to flee, a body blocked his path.

"Will." Tim looked down at him mournfully.

Will's eyes snapped open, and he found himself in his room, beneath his familiar ancient quilt. For a moment he wondered why Guernsey—his old Labrador retriever—wasn't curled up snoring at the end of his bed. Then Will remembered: Guernsey had been killed a few weeks ago. She had died trying to save him and Gretchen from a seekrieger—a bloodthirsty mermaid.

They had all nearly died. But then Gretchen had

changed and—somehow—had set the bay on fire, kill-
ing the seekriegers. Even Asia, who—though a Siren—
had been their friend.

Will's mind swam with the memory of Gretchen
that night—how her eyes had burned with red flame,
how she had spoken to him in a strange voice. And
then, once the seekriegers' shrieks had died away,
Gretchen had fainted, falling into the bay with a
small splash. Gretchen had no memory of setting the
fire. She didn't know that she had, briefly, become
someone—or some*thing*—else. And she didn't know
the truth about Asia.

These were secrets that Will was keeping.

He sighed, staring up at the ceiling, as the smell of
eggs frying in a pan wafted up to him. His body was
heavy; he wasn't sure he could get out of bed, even if
he wanted to. And he didn't want to. Why should he?
His brother had been killed in a boating accident the
summer before. His dog was dead. And his best friend
was . . . what?

A monster.

That word was ugly in his mind, but he couldn't
come up with anything else. *Creature,* perhaps. *Being.*

Will rolled over and pulled his quilt up to his shoulder. But his eyes were wide open—he wasn't sleepy. A
sound floated up to him dimly. It was a laugh. Gretch-
en's laugh. The sound chilled him, but it also made it
impossible for him to stay in bed.

Will tossed the covers aside and pressed his feet
against the wide pine planks of the floor. It was cold.
That wasn't surprising, given that it was September. It

could get quite chilly out on Long Island in the morning. Will yanked on a navy blue hoodie sweatshirt and staggered downstairs in his pajama bottoms.

Gretchen was facing away from him as he walked into the kitchen. She was seated at the wooden farm table, drinking coffee and eating eggs. Mr. Archer was standing beside the stove, spatula in hand.

"There you are," he said as Will stepped through the doorway. "Go get us some wood, will you? Let's get a fire started; it's cold in here." He reached over and expertly slipped the spatula under the eggs, flipping them with a flick of his wrist. Mr. Archer didn't cook much, but eggs were his specialty.

Gretchen gave Will a smile. "Hey, sheetface."

"Don't call me sheetface," Will replied automatically. This had been an in-joke with them since about sixth grade, when Gretchen had made an innocent reference to the fact that Will had creases smashed into his skin after sleeping facedown on a rumpled pillow. Tim had misheard it as profanity, and the whole thing had gotten them into trouble with their parents. "Are those eggs for me?" he asked his father.

"They could be, if you bring in that wood."

Will slipped his feet into the heavy boots he kept by the door and yanked the hood over his head. He pulled three logs from the top of the pile in the backyard, then trudged inside and threw them into the woodstove. There were still enough orange embers—the wood would flare up in a matter of moments.

"Get that door closed behind you," Mr. Archer told him.

"It's not supposed to be cold," Gretchen said as she polished off the eggs. "School doesn't even start for another three days."

"They got the new building done yet?" Mr. Archer asked, placing the second plate of eggs on the table.

Will shut the door and kicked off his boots. He sat down in front of the eggs and picked up a fork. "Not yet. Looks like we won't have an auditorium until spring."

"Government projects never finish on time." This was Mr. Archer's observation. He drained the rest of his coffee, then placed the mug on the counter. "I'll see you kids later." He strode out the door, letting in another blast of cool air.

Will looked up at Gretchen, who gave him a half-hearted smile. It was as if her cheerfulness had walked out the door with Mr. Archer. Her long blond hair was tied back in a ponytail, and wisps curled around her face. She looked disheveled in her running clothes. She was still beautiful, of course, but her usually restless body was subdued and still, and her skin seemed pale—like a piece of driftwood on the shore, bleached by sun and salt. "You okay?"

Gretchen shrugged. "Not looking forward to senior year."

Will snorted. "God, who is?" He didn't want to admit that he was. For the first time, Gretchen would be there. He'd have her for the whole year, not just the summer. He was surprised at the greediness of his friendship, the quickened pace of his heart when he thought about it.

"I'm not sure how I'm supposed to deal with something as . . . I don't know, banal as school." She put her fingers to her temples.

"Nice big word." Will dipped a piece of wheat toast into the yolk, letting it ooze onto his plate.

"Yeah—which reminds me, I need to take the SAT soon."

"Talk about banal."

"Seriously."

"It might be a relief, though. Give us something to do."

Gretchen seemed to think this over. "I guess."

"It'll keep us off the streets."

"Hopefully."

Will could see her pulse throbbing at the place where the delicate skin of her neck met her collarbone. A sheen of sweat highlighted the elegant curve of her throat. But her arms rested listlessly against the table and her long fingers picked slowly, aimlessly, at her napkin. Her blue eyes, usually lit with fire, seemed almost blank. "You look tired."

Gretchen smiled wryly. "Gee, thanks. You sure know how to make a girl feel special."

Will ignored her sarcasm. "You okay? Been sleep-walking?"

"Not since the hospital."

Gretchen had recovered in the hospital after that night when she had turned into that . . . thing. Will felt his chest tighten at the memory of Gretchen, how pale and young she had looked against the sterile white hospital sheets. He had been so scared—terrified of what might happen when she opened her eyes.

But then she woke up. And she had just been Gretchen. She hadn't remembered anything.

"You don't look too well yourself," she said to him.

Will cleared his throat. "Must be a case of senioritis."

"I hear that's going around."

Will nodded. The air felt heavy with all of the things he chose not to say. "It's pretty serious," he said.

"Mmm-hmm."

He studied the blankness in her eyes again, and wondered suddenly if there were secrets she was keeping, too.

Another blast of cool air announced the arrival of Will's uncle. "Hey!" Carl said as he stepped into the kitchen and tossed the newspaper onto the farm table. "Gretchen! Good to see you!" Carl leaned his beefy body to give Gretchen a warm hug. "Where's Bert?" he asked Will.

"Out in the greenhouses, most likely," Will said.

"You kids enjoying the scones?"

"World's best," Gretchen said brightly. Will smiled at her faintly, thinking how much she was like the moon—able to reflect the light cast on her by another source, but with a side always turned away, always hidden in shadow.

"Tell me about it!" Carl grabbed a currant scone from the plate on the counter, then took a bite out of it.

"Do you want some coffee?" Gretchen asked, just

as if this were her house and not Will's. "There's still some in the pot."

"No, thanks." He took another bite of scone, then winked at Will. "I guess I'd better get moving." He glanced at the paper, frowning slightly at the photo on the front page. The creases at the edges of his eyes deepened for a moment. But his expression changed so quickly that Will was hardly sure he'd seen it at all before it altered.

"I love your uncle—he's so warm," Gretchen observed as the door swung closed.

"He's a good guy," Will agreed, but he turned his eyes to look at the picture that had made his uncle frown. The front page had an article on the public beach closing for the season. The lifeguard chair sat empty, and off to the right, a lone person stood by the waves in a black T-shirt and jeans. "Your friend makes news again," Will announced, holding up the paper for Gretchen to see.

Gretchen looked at the photo, and he was certain that she recognized the figure as easily as he had. It was Kirk Worstler, town enigma.

"He's just going for a walk." Gretchen stabbed at her eggs, spearing the last mouthful. "People do that in September."

"It just seems . . . odd," Will admitted. He thought about all the times he'd seen Kirk's name in the newspaper over the summer in connection with strange actions: he'd broken into a church and played the organ, he'd set off the town alarm. "I guess everything he does seems odd to me."

"He's just a strange, sad kid, Will." Gretchen looked at him from across the table, her eyes steady. "Don't judge him."

Will looked down at the table, still feeling her gaze. *Don't judge.* But Will knew things about Kirk that Gretchen didn't. Like that his family was connected to the Sirens—his ancestor had been rescued by Asia, but they had been tormented by hearing the Sirens' songs ever since. This was another secret Will had kept.

Layers and layers of secrets, each like the skin of an onion. Peel one away, another is revealed. All part of the same whole.

After breakfast, Gretchen headed home to shower and change, and Will threw on his work clothes. He spent most of the day helping his father on the farm—feeding the chickens and picturesque sheep, harvesting late-season tomatoes and early squash, trimming the now-overgrown hedges at the corner of their property. In the late afternoon he took a break and borrowed his uncle Carl's truck to pick up the lawn mower from the hardware store in town. The old riding mower broke down fairly regularly, but Will's father was too cheap to get a new one, so he got a friend who worked at the hardware store to fix it.

Once he picked up the mower, Will decided to take a quick walk and look at the ocean. He found himself standing in the sand, watching as the sea beat its incessant rhythm against the shore. Will looked out past the waves to where the water was quiet, almost still.

There was a silver flash, and a large gray and white gull dove for the fish that had just dared to break the surface. Soon a few more birds joined the other, and wide gray wings circled and dove, the gulls pecking at the school below the water. Will squinted in the afternoon light. The air was light and cool, and bore the fall smell of burning leaves. It was a beautiful day, but Will felt as if he carried his own darkness with him.

Even under the bright sky, the water was inky dark, and Will couldn't help thinking about the lives it had claimed. His brother, Tim. Asia.

An image flashed in his mind—the first time he had seen Asia. The sky pelted the sea with rain, and the ocean raged beneath a storm, but she had walked straight into the water. Thinking he was preventing a suicide, Will had plunged in after her. But she had disappeared, the soft ropes of her black hair slipping beyond his fingers into the mysterious depths.

That was before he learned the truth about Asia— that she was a Siren, an immortal with a debt. She had to deliver someone to Calypso and her murderous band of seekriegers, who were bent on seeking bloody revenge on humanity. And the person Asia sought to deliver was Gretchen.

After centuries of living beneath the waves, Calypso could no longer fit in among humans. She could not find the Burning One herself, could not entice her to the water. Asia could.

But Asia had not been able to do it; she couldn't deliver Gretchen. In fact, at the last moment, she had saved Gretchen from Calypso and her band. Will had never been sure why. He thought it was perhaps because Asia and Will shared a connection. Asia had lost a beloved sister. Will had lost a beloved brother. And Asia knew that Gretchen was like a sister to him. In the end, she simply wasn't a murderer.

And so Asia went down into the sea, just as Tim had.

Will's throat constricted as he thought of her crystalline green eyes. In a strange way, he had loved her. She knew what it was like to lose someone . . . to be haunted by that loss. He had been drawn to the mystery of her.

A renegade wave crept toward his foot, and Will stepped back just in time to avoid wetting his boot. He was dressed in a dirty old T-shirt and jeans that redefined filth. His hiking boots were covered in mud.

He looked out over the water again, sucking in a deep lungful of salty air. Though he knew the sea was treacherous, it still felt clean to him. He loved being here, even after all that had happened. But he had to get home. Will had to mow the front patch of lawn before the light disappeared, and—of course—his mother would pitch a fit if he wasn't washed up in time for dinner.

Just as Will started away, something caught his eye. A movement. He turned back toward the sea. The fish must have moved on, because the gulls were nowhere in sight. The surface of the water was a fine blue line against the edge of the horizon.

And then he thought he saw it. Just for a moment—the half-moon shape of a head rising from the water.

But before the face broke the surface, it disappeared again.

Will's heart tightened, and—without thinking—he took a step forward, his boot splashing into the shallow water. The object appeared once again, and this time Will's chest felt empty, hollow. It was a buoy. Just a buoy.

He put a hand to his forehead, feeling the smooth scar tissue that crossed his face beneath his palm. "It's nothing," he muttered to himself.

Then he turned and slogged through the sand back to the truck, wondering if he should have told Gretchen the truth about Asia when he had the chance. But it was so much easier not to.

His heart sank when he saw the bright orange paper peeping from beneath an ancient windshield wiper. "Oh, crap."

Will sighed. He'd parked in a permit-only zone and had been fool enough to think that the town patrol wouldn't check after the end of the summer season. They never wrote up his motorcycle when he parked it by the private beach. "Damn."

His father was going to be furious now. He had warned Will a hundred times to be careful when he borrowed his uncle's truck. A few years back, Carl had gotten a few serious traffic violations. They were still on his record, and another permit infraction could mean a suspended license. Will shook his head, already hearing the lecture his father was going to deliver when he got home. The unsaid implication was always *Tim never would have let this happen*, even though Will was the careful brother, the one who avoided trouble.

I'll just have to go down to the station with Uncle Carl to get this sorted out, Will thought. He didn't mind paying the ticket. It wasn't that much money. He just didn't want his uncle to suffer for his mistake.

It's amazing how small decisions can have such huge consequences, Will mused. It was a lesson he learned over and over. The trouble was, you never knew in advance which decision would spark a backlash, or what the repercussion would be.

You never knew . . . until it was too late.

Chapter Three

From the Walfang Gazette
Boat Runs Aground in Fog

Heavy fog caused a local fishing boat, the *Steely Joan,* to run aground, resulting in a great deal of damage to the hull. "I've been fishing these waters for twenty-seven years," said *Steely Joan* captain John Wood, "and I've never seen fog conditions like this." Local meteorologists are at a loss to explain what seems to be unusual weather for this time of year. . . .

"You're looking tired," Angel said as Gretchen reached for the platters laden with club sandwiches he had just placed in the window that separated the kitchen from the counter area at Bella's Diner. "Why don't you go on home?"

"Why does everyone keep saying that? I'm fine, Angel."

"You're pale. Like you're gonna fall over or something." He twitched his red mustache impatiently. "I don't want to have to pay out workers' compensation."

Gretchen gave him a wry smile. "Thanks for caring," she said. Weaving through the crowded diner, she hauled the platters over to table seventeen, a sullen mother-daughter pair. They looked almost identical, and Gretchen wondered how much of that was because of the identical expressions they wore. "Enjoy," Gretchen said brightly, but the women didn't even look up.

From the next table, Lisette gave Gretchen a wink with spidery fake eyelashes. The retro-punk head waitress had dyed her bangs purple and the rest of her hair black, and wore heavy navy eye shadow and diamond-studded cat's-eye glasses. She looked more like a rock star than like a person who ran a diner with the precision of a general and the personality of a cheerful Muppet, but looks could be deceiving.

Gretchen grabbed a pitcher of ice water and refilled the glasses at table thirteen. She checked in on the group in the booth, and tore out a check for the couple finishing up at the two-top near the window. Her actions were mechanical, automatic. That was what she liked about her work—she had to keep moving, but she didn't really have to think. Waitressing turned her into a robot, which was exactly what she wanted at that moment.

"Need a refill?" Gretchen asked, indicating the empty soda glass on the Formica table.

Kirk Worstler's large, dark eyes were trained on the open notebook before him. It was your typical spiral-bound, college-ruled Walmart special, but Kirk was using it as a sketchbook. "No, thanks," he whispered to the page. His arms were wrapped around the notebook in a protective posture.

Gretchen tried to peek into the center, where the shadow of his arm obscured the image he had been creating for the past hour. "May I see?" she asked.

Reluctantly Kirk leaned back, revealing the page. It was a picture of a woman, her head half out of the water. The lines were loose; ink blots smeared the page. In the margins, notes were scrawled in an uneven hand. The style was loose and unsophisticated. Still, there was something arresting about the image. The woman's eyes were in shadow, which gave the viewer the eerie sensation of being watched. Gretchen shivered a little.

"You hate it," Kirk said.

"No. It's good."

"But you still hate it."

There wasn't much Gretchen could say to this.

Kirk was a skinny kid, and his pale skin and lanky limbs made his body seem younger than sixteen. But his sad, watchful expression made his face look older. "You're an artist," he said after a moment.

"I like to draw."

"That's what an artist is."

"Then I guess I am. I guess we both are."

"No." Kirk pressed his palm against the page. "I don't like to draw much. But my therapist says it's good for me." He shrugged. "I don't really know what else to do, I guess. So I'm doing it."

Gretchen shifted her weight awkwardly. "That's good." It was no secret that Kirk had been pretty crazy for a while. But lately he'd seemed much better. Still wary, still eccentric . . . but better.

Kirk dug into his pocket and pulled out a crumpled dollar bill. He tossed it on the table, then dug around

again, finally coming up with a quarter and six nick-
els. He blushed. "I don't have a tip."

"Soda's only a dollar fifty."

"Five cents. Some tip."

"All I did was bring you a Coke. Seems fair."

Kirk bit his lip, then picked up his pen and went
back to his drawing, darkening the shadows on one of
the rocks.

"What, that kid has no order?" Angel snarled as
Gretchen slipped behind the counter. "This isn't the
public library. Tell him to order something or get out.
He can't just sit here drinking a Coke for five hours
every day."

Gretchen frowned. "He did order something, actually." She scribbled on her pad and handed it over.
"Medium-well."

Angel lifted an eyebrow at her. "Lucky for him," he
grumbled as he slung a hamburger patty onto the grill.

Gretchen didn't flinch. "Yeah. I guess he's hungry
tonight."

It's worth it, Gretchen told herself as she thought
of the cost of the burger, which would have to come
out of her tips. *Kirk isn't hurting anybody. He should
be allowed to just sit and work in peace.* After all, it
wasn't his fault that his parents were screwups and
that he had to live with his sister. It wasn't his fault
they were broke.

"Gretchen, sweetheart, I need you." Lisette pushed
her purple bangs out of her eyes. "Would you be a doll
and bus table nineteen? We've got people waiting."

"No problem." Gretchen cleared the table and wiped it down, then smiled at the mom and two young sons who took the booth. "Your waitress will be right with you," she said as she set paper placemats and silverware in front of them.

"Thanks, hon," Lisette called as she made her way over to the table.

Gretchen smiled. Lisette's cheerful demeanor was such a contrast to Angel's grouchy simplicity. And yet they were engaged. Despite a twenty-year age difference, despite completely contrasting sensibilities, they had fallen for each other.

"Order up!" Angel called.

Gretchen took the plate loaded with fries and punctuated with a hamburger, then reached for a glass and filled it with ice and Coke. She placed the order in front of a surprised-looking Kirk and announced, "On the house."

"Why?"

"Why not?"

Kirk thought this over. He took a fry and nibbled the end. Then he looked over Gretchen's shoulder, as if someone might be on his way over to snatch the food away. He took a bite of the burger and smiled up at Gretchen. He looked like an eight-year-old, a giddy kid.

"Order up, Lisette!" Angel shouted.

Lisette touched Gretchen's shoulder. "Would you take that for me, hon? I'm overloaded."

"Sure." Gretchen delivered the dessert to the booth by the door, then took care of her own tables. Now that Kirk had a plate of food in front of him, she could ignore him for a while. She didn't need to check in with him to make sure everything was all right. He was one customer who wouldn't complain.

Gretchen wrote out a few checks and started clearing tables. Then she filled up the dishwasher and started a load.

"Hey, hey, what do you say?" Angus McFarlan asked as he burst through the door. He grinned at Gretchen and perched on a stool and let his long arms flop across the counter. Everything about Angus was casual and graceless, which often served to hide his keen intelligence.

Gretchen smiled at her friend. "Hey, Angus. What brings you here?"

"Pie," Angus admitted. "And I had to clear my stuff out of my cubicle at the *Gazette*." Angus had been working at the local newspaper all summer.

"Internship's over?"

"Sadly, yes. But I'm going to see if I can still do a little newspapering in my spare time. If anything interesting comes across my path. Like, maybe I'll do an article on pie."

"Cherry, strawberry-rhubarb, blueberry, or lemon meringue."

"No apple?"

"Sold out."

"Strawberry-rhubarb, then."

"Whipped cream?"

"Double dose."

Gretchen served up a thick wedge of the pie,

heaped a small mountain of white cream on top, and handed it over.

"This is insane," Lisette griped as she staggered back toward the counter, her tray loaded down with dirty platters and cups. "Angel, we need another waitress."

"Not during the off season."

"Angel! Do you see anything off about this diner?" Lisette put down the tray and gestured to the busy restaurant. True, the dinner hour had already peaked, but plenty of customers were still eating or lingering to chat. Bella's appealed to the local crowd, not the tourists. Even on a Thursday, there were customers at the dinner hour.

"You've got Gretchen."

"Gretchen's only here one night during the week and on weekends! I can't handle this whole place by myself."

"You'll be able to in January."

"That's what you said last year, and we were still busy," Lisette shot back. "At least hire a busboy."

"What about Kirk?" Gretchen suggested. The words surprised her, but she had to admit that it made sense. Kirk was lonely. Kirk needed money.

"Kirk?" Angel glared at her. "He's crazy."

"Well then, he's qualified to work here," Angus put in. Angel glowered at him from beneath thick eyebrows, and Angus got back to work on his pie.

"He isn't crazy," Gretchen insisted. "He's much better. Besides, he's always here."

"Does he have any experience?" Lisette asked.

"I doubt it," Gretchen admitted.

"Hm. Well, I'll go talk to him," Lisette volunteered.

"What?" Angel scoffed. "You can't be serious."

"Watch this," Lisette snapped, and started over toward Kirk's table.

"That woman." Angel shook his head with a mixture of fury and reverence.

Gretchen watched as Kirk listened, wide-eyed, then nodded. *Done deal,* she said to herself. *Kirk needs something in his life,* she mused. *Something besides the weird images in his mind.*

"You did a good deed," Angus said, scooping up the last of his pie.

She sighed, smiling. She didn't question why helping Kirk made her so happy.

Maybe she should have, but she didn't.

Chapter Four

*Will looked down at the lake from the
top of the bluff. Overhead, a full moon
gleamed at its twin, which shimmered in
the calm, dark water below. At one end
were dunes. Closer by were hulking
black rocks.*

*Will sat watching the water, fighting
the feeling of unease that crept over him.
He couldn't shake the sensation that
something was in the water.
Something . . . dark.*

*All at once, one of the black rocks
stretched, revealing a long neck, an
angular head. It shifted its weight onto
its muscular legs and ambled down to
the black water. It bent toward the water
as if it might drink, and then—with a
single breath—the dragon set the
surface of the bay on fire. Flames rose
toward the sky, and smoke choked Will's
lungs. The water burned and burned,
and Will realized that the water wasn't
the sea at all, but a lake of oil. It went
on burning, and the dragon waded into
the lake of fire. It made no sound as the
fire consumed it, but just went on staring
at Will with orange eyes that looked like
lit coal.*

Will didn't remember the dream as he let the warm
water wash over him. All that remained was a slightly

ill feeling, a mild unease that he couldn't name, like
the slimy track left by a snail. Steam rose around him,
and he let the water warm him to the bone, penetrat-
ing his tense muscles.

He thought about seeing the buoy the day before,
how it had unnerved him. Will wasn't the kind of person who saw things that weren't there. Even as a small
child, he had never believed in monsters or aliens or
supernatural creatures. That was why his brush with
the Sirens had taken him so wholly by surprise. After
Tim died, Will found he was unable to remember what
happened the night Tim disappeared—even though
Will was the only witness. They had taken out the boat
together. And then . . . a black hole.

The fact that he couldn't remember had become a
chink, a slight crack in his reasonable, ordered universe, and it had been just enough to allow for the
reality of the seekriegers to burst in, upending everything he thought he knew about reality.

Now he wondered how much of the world he had
ever really understood.

The knobs squeaked as he turned off the water,
and he ran his hands through his wet, shaggy hair. He
was still postponing getting a haircut. Will didn't like
looking at the scar that sliced across his face, and his
long sandy mane hid it.

Water dripped across his chest, finding a channel
in the groove between his defined abdominal muscles.
A summer of working on the farm had given him a
tan, toned body, but he was completely unself-
conscious as he wrapped a towel low on his hips.

He stepped onto the rug and flicked a glance at the fogged-up mirror before pulling open the medicine cabinet. Razor, shaving cream, toothbrush, toothpaste. He shut it again.

The mirror faced him, a word scrawled into the gray condensation. *FURY.*

With a gasp, he turned and opened the door to his empty room beyond. He held still, taut as a bowstring, but nothing moved. There was no sound. He turned back to the mirror.

But the word had disappeared; the mirror was clear. Steam had rushed out the door when he opened it, and the bathroom was already growing chill.

Slowly Will closed the door. Feeling as if his body were filled with lead, he sat down on the edge of the bathtub. *FURY.*

His mind couldn't take any meaning from the word, could hardly even admit that it existed. *You imagined it,* his brain whispered.

But his heart was racing and fear coursed through his veins like poison. He knew from experience that he didn't have to believe it for it to be real.

A few hours later Will sat at the farm stand, looking at the pile of butternut squash, sprawled like lazy sea lions across the wide wooden table. A few sugar pumpkins lined the short edge of the table beside some early yellow-and-green-striped delicata. Dark green dinosaur kale was tucked beside sultry red beets.

Late summer had always been Will's favorite time of year at his family's farm stand. It had been Tim's favorite, too. Both brothers loved the soups and stews their mother would make from the abundant winter squash. The air was sweet and cool, and the clientele changed from manic, ever-texting Manhattanites to neighbors and local restaurateurs.

Every year Tim would wait eagerly for the first of the sugar pumpkins. He was famous for his pumpkin pie, which was equal parts spicy and sweet. Their grandmother Archer had refused to give the recipe to Evelyn, her daughter-in-law, and instead passed the secret to Tim, who took pie baking seriously. Will touched the firm orange flesh of one of the pumpkins, wishing he had that recipe. But both of the people who knew it were dead now.

A gentle wind picked up, and Will heard a sound like his brother's laugh. He looked up. The wind chime at the end of the shed let out a low ringing tone. The sky overhead was turning gray.

"Will!"

Will blinked, swallowing hard to open his closed throat. He managed to smile at Gretchen, who was walking down the driveway. Her golden hair hung loose around her face, and she was wearing a faded red T-shirt and jeans. Another sign of fall—Gretchen's long legs were covered. She hoisted herself onto her usual perch at the end of the heavy wooden cash register table.

"What's wrong?" Will asked.

Gretchen cocked her head. "What? Nothing—why?"

Will shrugged. "I don't know. Everything okay?"

Gretchen shook her head. She looked up the road,

where a half-rusted Ford was making its way toward the farm stand. "Here comes Angus," she said, half to herself.

There was something in her tone that Will couldn't read. It didn't help that he had lost his hearing in one ear the summer before. It meant that he heard most things as if they were being spoken through a thick wad of cotton.

Angus pulled up and got out of his battered Ford, carefully locking it before he walked over to the stand. "Greetings, friends! And others." He grinned at Will and shoved his mop of curly brown hair out of his eyes. "So, has Gretchen filled you in on her philan-thropy last night?"

Will looked over at Gretchen, who was flashing Angus a threatening glower.

"Aaannnd . . . I just said something I wasn't sup-posed to," Angus said.

"What? What are we talking about?" Will demanded.

Gretchen shrugged. "I got Kirk a job at the diner. No big deal."

Will sighed, sitting down on the edge of the table. "Kirk Worstler?"

Gretchen came over and touched his shoulder. "What's wrong? I know you don't like him, but he's not that weird."

Will looked into her face—those chameleon-like green-blue eyes. It wasn't the fact that he was weird that bothered Will. It was the fact that weird things happened around him. He was like a canary in a coal mine that way. But he didn't want to get into it. "Okay," he said at last. But he couldn't shake the feeling that Kirk's presence was an ill omen. Several weeks ago, when Kirk was in the thick of one of his crazy moments, he had told Will, "The fury must awaken."

FURY.

Something wet brushed against Will's cheek, and he looked up. It was a raindrop. Dark clouds had moved in. The sun was still burning behind them, sending out golden light at the edges, but the darkness was gathering. "It's about to rain," Will said.

"Well, we'd better get inside," Angus pointed out. "No use getting drenched."

"Yeah," Will agreed, but he was looking at Gretchen. "It's not like we can stop it."

Chapter Five

From The Eumenides, *by Aeschylus*

Hear the hymn of hell,
O'er the victim sounding.
Chant of frenzy, chant of ill,
Sense and will confounding!
Round the soul entwining
Without lute or lyre—
Soul in madness pining,
Wasting as with fire.

"Hold on," Gretchen said as she plowed the Gremlin through a massive puddle, sending a sheet of water over a fence rail at the edge of the road. "Sorry," she muttered.

"What could you have done about it?" Will asked, which was a reasonable question, in Gretchen's opinion. The puddle had stretched entirely across the street, even flooding part of the lush green lawn. Rain poured from the dark gray sky as if it wanted to signal the official end to summer and the start of the gloomy fall.

Perfect day to start my senior year, Gretchen thought. Still, she was glad to be heading to school in a comfortable pair of jeans and a long-sleeved T-shirt instead of the plaid skirt and button-down white oxford that had been the uniform at her all-girls academy in Manhattan. And she was glad to be with Will, under the protection of her vintage Gremlin, instead of alone, struggling with an umbrella as she walked the fourteen blocks from her apartment to the Standish School.

This morning she'd yanked some clothes from the boxes that had been delivered the day before, pulled them on, and tumbled outside toward her car. It seemed like a strangely informal way to start the day.

The wind picked up, howling in rage as the Gremlin made its way over the bridge. Lightning flashed over the water and thunder rumbled. Gretchen let out a grunt as she struggled with the steering wheel, fighting to keep a straight course. Her heart strained against her chest. She tried not to imagine plunging over the edge, beating her fists against the window as the car filled with water. . . .

"Strong wind," Will said.

Gretchen nodded, keeping her eyes on the wet asphalt. She breathed easier as they reached the other side of the bridge and headed down a tree-lined lane.

"Here. Turn here," Will said. "Left."

"Already?" But Gretchen was following orders, taking the sharp left at the intersection.

"Now right," Will instructed. "We'll come in the rear parking lot. Front one is always packed. You'll never get a spot."

Gretchen nodded, and—sure enough—in a moment the playing fields at the rear of the school came into view. Gretchen cruised around the parking lot slowly, waiting patiently as the car in front of her pulled into a spot. They were late. The parking lot was packed with cars but nearly empty of people. Everyone had gotten to school early. *Best foot forward,* Gretchen thought. *For them.*

A dark, hooded figure darted through the rain, toward the glass double doors. *Kirk.* Gretchen wondered what he thought of school. She was sort of surprised to see him going to class just like a normal person.

In the end, the only available parking spot was between two oversized SUVs. Gretchen pulled in carefully. "Do you have enough room to get out?"

Will peered out the window. "Barely," he said.

The wind howled again as Will reached over the rear of his seat for his backpack. "Grab my umbrella— it's in the backseat," Gretchen said as she yanked open the handle and ducked into the rain. The wind blew harder, splattering her skin as it flew at her sideways.

The bell rang just as they hurried through the double doors. Water lay across the floor, and wet tracks led down the hall. A few students still loitered near lockers or strode past doorways, looking for classes. Gretchen pulled her damp class schedule from her bag. "Where am I going?" she asked, showing the limp paper to Will.

"That's right down the hall." Will pointed it out to her. "Third door on the right."

"Where's yours?" Gretchen asked.

"English is in the other wing. I'd better haul."

Gretchen bit her lip and gave Will a half wave as he

hurried in the other direction. Until she saw him rushing away, she hadn't realized just how much comfort it gave her to know he was there. She was hit with another sense of vertigo, similar to the one she'd had going over the bridge. She didn't like the thought of him being in the other wing. She wanted to keep him close.

Gretchen turned toward her class, remembering the moment a few weeks earlier when she had awoken in the hospital. Will had been there. He had kissed her on the forehead, and the soft touch of his lips had sent warmth through her whole body.

She had loved Will for years, but it was a love that almost frightened her with its intensity and implications. That was why she often sought out other boyfriends—guys who were fun but didn't mean much to her. Like Jason Detenber. He was smart and handsome, but he'd had a mean streak.

Class had already started by the time Gretchen arrived at advanced-placement chemistry. She stood in the doorway, waiting for the teacher to look up. Blood was still pounding in her ears, and she felt hot, despite being drenched to the skin. She shivered, although she wasn't cold.

The teacher stood before a whiteboard, already talking about the requirements for labs. She was petite, and wore rimless glasses before large brown eyes. Her close-cropped hair and tailored clothes told Gretchen that she was the organized type, someone who would hand out a syllabus and expect all assignments on time—no excuses.

"Mrs. Hoover?"

"It's Ms.," the teacher corrected automatically, a fraction of a second before her eyebrows lifted archly. *Looking my best,* Gretchen thought wryly as the teacher's face registered surprise at Gretchen's disheveled appearance.

A murmur ran through the class.

"May I help you?" Ms. Hoover asked, as if Gretchen couldn't possibly be one of her students.

Gretchen walked in and handed her teacher the schedule. "I'm in this class."

Ms. Hoover read it, sighed, and looked at Gretchen. "Okay, there's a seat at the back. We're reviewing our equipment."

Gretchen nodded and made her way to a table at the back, where a girl with long brown-black hair and golden skin sat beside an empty lab stool. As Gretchen passed, the other students smirked and snickered, but her lab partner just nodded as Gretchen slid onto the stool. She didn't seem at all surprised or disturbed by Gretchen's appearance. As the dark-haired girl surveyed her face with mysterious black eyes, Gretchen was hit with a sudden, stabbing headache, and she put her fingers to her temples. It subsided as suddenly as it had arrived, and Gretchen raked her fingers through her damp hair, trying to force it into some sort of order.

"Now I'd like you to take a moment to inventory and explore your equipment," Ms. Hoover announced. "I'm passing out a list of everything that should be at your station." She gave a stack of papers to a good-looking guy in a letterman's jacket, who handed a list to someone at each table. "Make sure it's all in working order. Our first lab is on Wednesday, and I don't want to hear any excuses."

Gretchen was fighting a persistent sense of unreality—trying to jam thoughts that didn't go together into her mind all at once.

"Who's your new lab partner, Mafer?" the letterman asked as he handed her an inventory sheet. He had cocoa skin and a brilliant smile, and Gretchen was sure that he was used to having every female in a ten-mile radius sigh over him.

"Her name's Gretchen," Mafer replied.

Gretchen cocked her head. "How did you know?"

"Mafer knows all," the letterman joked. He flashed a killer smile at Gretchen before heading off to his table.

Gretchen placed her hands on the table, trying to steady herself. "No, seriously, how did you know?"

"I'm psychic," Mafer said. "Also, Ms. Hoover called roll. You were the only one who wasn't here." Her dark eyes were large and liquid, and her glance was cut with keen intelligence. There was something about Mafer that made her seem ancient. Gretchen shifted in her chair, uncomfortable.

"Oh. Right."

Mafer held up the paper. "Should we run down this list? Want to see if all of the proper tongs are in the proper drawer?"

"Sure."

Mafer read out the list of supplies, and Gretchen checked to make sure they were in the drawer. Everything was in excellent condition; nothing was missing.

"So, what kind of name is Mafer?" Gretchen asked when her lab partner pulled out the beakers. "Does it have a meaning?"

"It's a nickname—short for Maria Fernanda. Maria Fernanda Aguilar Echevarria."

"Why would you want to shorten that?" Gretchen joked.

"Right." A dry smile. "My grandparents are from Mexico."

"Were you born in Walfang?"

"No, Chicago. But my mom's on a deployment. My brother and I have been living with my grandmother in Waterbreak. How did you end up here?"

How did *I end up here?* It was a good question, one with a complicated answer. "My dad and I have always spent summers out here. He decided we should move out full-time."

"You're close to him."

"Yeah." Gretchen smiled at the thought of Johnny. It was funny to think that he would come in for a parent-teacher conference with buttoned-down Ms. Hoover. *Wonder what she'll think of him,* Gretchen thought.

"So—are you feeling better?"

"Better?"

"You seemed upset when you came in. Are you okay now?"

The thought of the howling wind, the journey over the bridge, made Gretchen's heart pound again.

Mafer must have read her face, because she said, "Sorry."

"No, I—" Gretchen shook her head. "I just don't like water much."

Mafer nodded, sympathetic but unsurprised, and waited a moment, as if inviting her to say more. But Gretchen didn't want to say more. She just focused on calming her breaths, making them even. Fifteen seconds ticked by, and Mafer handed Gretchen a box of matches and nodded at the Bunsen burner. "Let's light this thing up."

Gretchen checked to make sure that the holes in the burner were closed. Then she lit the match.

Gretchen pushed the button, then turned on the gas tap and held out the light. The burner lit, then flared unexpectedly, sending up a gout of flame. She shrieked as the edge of her sleeve caught fire.

The class erupted into chaos—everyone yelling at once—as Gretchen waved her flaming arm before her face. Mafer grabbed the sweater from the back of her chair and tossed it over Gretchen's arm, then turned off the gas.

"What happened?" Ms. Hoover ran over, shouting. "What did you do?"

"Gretchen is going to the nurse," Mafer announced. She took Gretchen's other elbow and started to lead her out of the classroom. The students cleared a path for them. It flashed into Gretchen's mind that her classmates were a little afraid of Mafer.

"Yes. Yes, of course." Ms. Hoover looked serious. "Okay, everybody back to work. Nobody come near this burner."

The noise subsided as the door to Ms. Hoover's class shut behind them.

"It doesn't hurt," Gretchen said.

"You're in shock."

Gretchen followed obediently as Mafer drew her away from the door. "Just down the hall," Mafer said before Gretchen could ask the question. They walked to a small door, and Mafer pulled it open. A bored-looking overweight woman looked up from her desk.

"This girl probably needs to go to the hospital," Mafer said. "She's got a bad burn."

"What?" The nurse hurried over to Gretchen. Her large hands were gentle as she pulled away the red sweater wrapped around her arm. The sleeve of her orange shirt was charred. Gingerly the nurse peeled the fabric away from Gretchen's arm.

The skin was pink, completely unharmed. The nurse pushed the fabric up further, and Gretchen held up her whole arm. There was no sign that the fire had ever touched her.

Gretchen looked at Mafer, whose eyebrows lifted slightly.

"You're lucky," the nurse said after a moment. "You put it out in time. It just caught your sleeve."

Gretchen stared at her charred sleeve. How had she escaped getting hurt?

"So . . . should we just head back to class?" Mafer asked. "I mean, she was just on fire."

The nurse looked at her sternly. "*You* can go back to class. This one has to fill out an injury form."

Mafer put a gentle hand on Gretchen's shoulder. When Gretchen looked up, they locked eyes for a moment. "Are you okay?"

"I guess," Gretchen said. She didn't really know the answer.

Mafer nodded. "All right. Take it easy. Go home after this. It's just the first day—you won't miss anything."

"She can't just go home," the nurse said primly.

"Oh, come on." Mafer shook her head and walked out the door.

The nurse frowned after her, then stood up and turned toward a large black filing cabinet. "Name?"

"Gretchen Ellis."

The nurse flipped to the *E*'s and pulled out a folder. She flipped it open, then frowned. "This isn't complete."

"It isn't?"

With a snap, the nurse pulled the paperwork from the file. "Your parents forgot to fill out some of their medical history." She handed it to Gretchen. "Please bring this back to me tomorrow, along with the signed injury report." She sat down heavily in the office chair and pulled a blank form from a drawer.

Gretchen looked down at the paperwork in her hands. Her mind swam, and she had to lean back on the table.

"Are you all right?" the nurse asked.

"Not really," Gretchen replied.

The nurse came over and touched Gretchen's hair. It was a kind gesture, almost motherly, and it left

Gretchen feeling tired. "Maybe you *should* go home," the nurse said after a moment. "You've had a scare. Do you have a ride?"

Gretchen nodded. She had her car. Not that she wanted to face the journey over the bridge alone, not with the howling wind outside. Besides, she didn't want to strand Will at school. She let out a sigh. "It's the first day," she said at last. "I think I'll stay."

"Hey." Will smiled at her warmly and indicated the seat across from his.

A few hours had passed, but Gretchen was still getting over her scare from the morning. It was good to see Will, though. Peace settled over Gretchen as she took the seat by the window. Outside, the rain had quieted to a steady patter, the clouds lining the sky with a smooth blanket of gray. The weather didn't seem menacing anymore. Here, tucked in the corner of the crowded cafeteria with Will, it somehow seemed cozy to have a dreary day outside.

"So, how's the first day going?" Will asked.

"Oh—not too bad." Gretchen pressed her lips together in something she hoped resembled a smile. "Although I'm starting to wonder why I'm taking all of these AP courses."

"Because you're a glutton for punishment?" Will suggested.

"It's starting to look that way."

"Hey, guys!" Angus descended on them with his usual ton-of-bricks suavity, dropping into the seat beside Will and letting his tray clatter on the table. "So, what's all this about catching fire?"

Gretchen hid her face in her hands as Will let out a strangled *"What?"*

"It's nothing—my sleeve got caught in a Bunsen burner."

"So!" Angus pulled a notebook out of his back pocket. "Are you going to sue the school, or what?"

Gretchen rolled her eyes. "Get serious."

"I am! Word on the street is that you want to take the school district to court for unsafe building practices and faulty lab equipment."

"That is a complete fabrication."

"No comment," Angus said, writing on his pad.

Will glowered at his friend and twisted the notebook out of his hand.

"Hey!" Angus protested.

"Find another story." Will swiveled in his seat and tossed the notebook into a nearby trash can.

"You know, that had my homework assignments in it," Angus told him.

"It's only the first day of school, Angus," Will pointed out. "See if you can remember."

"Seriously, Gretchen, would you consider doing an interview with the paper?" Angus asked. "Even just a first-person I'm-so-lucky-to-be-alive kind of deal?"

"Angus, I'm already the new girl—I'm not looking for attention," Gretchen said. "I just want to blend in a little."

Angus laughed. "Good luck." He nodded over at

someone sitting in the corner, peering at Gretchen over the top of a notebook.

"Kirk doesn't count." Gretchen's voice was soft. Kirk smiled at her with a sweet, innocent grin. He reminded her of a pet, or a little brother, or something.

"Yeah, he's always had the stares for you," Angus admitted.

Will shuddered. "God, he gives me the creeps."

"There's nothing wrong with him," Gretchen said as Kirk went back to sketching.

"Except that he's crazy and potentially dangerous," Angus said brightly.

"He isn't dangerous," Gretchen protested.

"You don't know that. He's unstable, at least." Will looked at her closely. "I don't want you hanging around him, Gretchen."

"Ah, news flash, Will." Gretchen's voice was heavy with sarcasm. "You're not my dad."

"No, because your dad wouldn't even try to make any rules, would he?"

"What are you saying about my father?" Gretchen demanded. She realized that she must have looked pretty intimidating just then, because Angus leaned forward.

"Okay, let's not bring parents into any of this," he said. "Let's just all take some nice, cleansing breaths—"

"Shut up, Angus," Will snapped.

For a moment nobody knew what to say. The silence was broken by the bell signaling the end of lunch.

"I've got to get my stuff for my next class," Gretchen

said, jamming her lunch into the bag. She pushed back her chair and started toward the door. "See you, Angus," she called over her shoulder as she joined the general exodus from the cafeteria.

"Nice going," she heard Angus say to Will.

Gretchen's mind was fogged with irritation, and it took her three tries to open her combination lock. It finally gave way with a yank, and she slammed her books inside.

"I don't want to have to report you to the Society for the Prevention of Cruelty to Literature," said a voice.

Gretchen looked up. Mafer was leaning against the metal locker beside hers, grinning.

"Be nice to the books," Mafer said.

Gretchen sighed. "I'm just—"

"Pissed at someone?" Mafer guessed.

Gretchen's mouth twisted into a half smile. "How could you tell?"

"Lovers' quarrel?" Mafer asked.

Gretchen felt her face flush hot. "What?" She tried to laugh, but it came out strangled. "No!"

Mafer shrugged. "Okay."

"Don't say okay like that. Like you know something. Which you don't."

"Okay."

Gretchen breathed out an exasperated sigh.

"Boys and girls can be friends, right?" Mafer said brightly. "It always works like that."

"It can," Gretchen said.

Mafer looked down the hall, where Will had

reappeared. He was drifting slowly toward class beside Angus. "He's that boy . . ." Her voice went soft, almost dreamlike. "The one who went crazy when his brother died. What was his name?" She closed her eyes. "Timothy Archer."

Gretchen stared at her. "Will didn't go crazy."

"No?" Mafer opened them again, her dark eyes frank yet languid.

"He's not crazy. Not at all."

"Let me tell you a little secret." Mafer leaned in close enough so that Gretchen could smell the slight almond scent of her hair, the mint of her breath. "Everybody around here's a little crazy." She pulled back and looked Gretchen full in the face.

Gretchen didn't know what to say. Her head was spinning. *I've been locked in an asylum,* she thought. *Trapped with the lunatics.*

"So, when can we get together to talk about our project?" Mafer asked. Just like that. As if they had been passing the time or talking about the weather. It took a moment for Gretchen's thoughts to realign.

"Project?"

"Hoover assigned a report, due before our lab next Wednesday. It's about matter. When can you get together?" Mafer chewed on the end of her blue pen.

"I—I don't know," Gretchen stammered. "Tomorrow afternoon?"

"Perfect." Mafer scribbled a note on the back of her hand. "See you in class, lab partner." And then she walked off down the hall just as the first bell rang.

Lockers slammed and students began to race toward classes. Gretchen glanced around at the other normal-looking kids and wondered where Kirk had disappeared to.

Everybody around here's a little crazy, Mafer had said.

Gretchen was starting to believe it.

She turned and found herself staring right into the front of Angus's blue-checked button-down shirt. He smiled at her, shoving his floppy curls to one side. "So you're hanging with the witch now?"

"What?"

"Bayshore Regional's very own resident witch," Angus said with an indifferent shrug. He leaned in to whisper dramatically, "She's got *powers,*" then waggled his eyebrows in what Gretchen guessed was supposed to convey significance.

"Like what?" Gretchen demanded.

"Like Abigail Noyes stole her boyfriend last year." Angus studied his fingernails. "And ended up with a broken arm."

"Mafer broke her arm?" Gretchen was having trouble imagining the petite girl getting violent.

"No, Abigail broke it in cheerleading practice," Angus admitted. "But she said it was because Mafer worked some voodoo shit on her."

"That is the dumbest thing I've ever heard," Gretchen said simply.

"And in the eighth grade, there was some intense Ouija board debacle at Sarah Gutten's birthday party.

The girls swear Mafer was moving that thing with her mind, and Sarah thought she saw the ghost of her dead grandmother."

"Now there's a *new* dumbest thing I've ever heard. Keep it up, Angus, you're going for a record."

"I'm telling you, she sees dead people."

"So now *you're* trying to tell me who to be friends with? Are you and Will some kind of committee?"

"Oh, no way! I think she's cool. And really good-looking." He grinned. "And my opinion is that if she's a witch, it's way better to have her as a friend than as an enemy, am I right? I'm just telling you that she has a rep, because who else is going to tell you?"

Gretchen shook her head, but she actually found a laugh buried in her chest. She put a hand on Angus's arm. "Okay, thanks."

"Don't mention it," Angus said.

The bell rang, releasing them, and Gretchen headed off to her next class, more certain than ever that everyone around her really was insane, after all.

"What do you want? What can I get you?" Johnny ran his hand through his mop of dark hair, then rubbed his long sideburn. "You want soup? I can go to the store."

"I'm not sick, Dad."

Johnny responded by pulling a blanket over her. Bananas hopped onto the couch beside Gretchen, then started worrying her claws on the throw pillow. "You're no help," Johnny scolded the cat.

Bananas flicked her orange and white tail.

"I could go rent some movies. Maybe something funny."

Gretchen sighed. *Why did I give him the accident report?* she wondered. It was nice that her dad cared about her, but it was times like this that made her wish he had a regular job, so he could go off to work and leave her alone for a while. "Maybe I'll make some tea."

"Lie back." Johnny pointed at her. "I'll make the tea. What kind do you want?"

"Mint something."

"Do we have that?"

Gretchen started to haul herself off the couch. "I'll make it."

"No! Sit." Johnny picked up the remote control and clicked on the television. "I'll be back in a minute." He bustled off to the kitchen.

Gretchen settled back onto the couch, and the cat stepped gingerly onto her lap, kneading her stomach with soft paws. Gretchen scratched her behind the ears, and Bananas settled down and began to purr.

Drawers opened and banged closed in the kitchen, which made Gretchen smile. Johnny was having trouble finding the tea. He was a coffee guy.

The television blared on, showing a couple as they remodeled their bathroom. Gretchen clicked it off.

Johnny hadn't taken the news about the Bunsen burner well. He'd had a haunted expression on his face as he signed the release form and he'd made her show him her arm right away. He wasn't reassured by the pink skin. It was as if all he could see was the blackened shirt sleeve, the measure of how bad the accident could have been.

The rain had died away, leaving a gray sky above and wet asphalt below. The air was calm, almost holding its breath, and beyond the window the orange and yellow leaves seemed to pop against the sky. He'd put his arm around her and pulled her into a hug. "You must have been so scared," he'd whispered into her hair.

Gretchen had shaken her head. "I wasn't."

Johnny had looked at her, then pulled away and peered deeply into her eyes, as if he were searching for something.

"Mint Magic," Johnny said as he walked back into the living room, carrying a steaming mug. He had chosen one with a reindeer on it, a Christmas gift from Gretchen to her mother long ago. Yvonne had left it behind when she moved out. "I hope it's strong enough."

Gretchen accepted the cup gratefully. "Thanks." She placed it on the coffee table, causing Bananas to hop off her lap and strut away.

Johnny sat in the armchair and looked at Gretchen expectantly, as if he were awaiting instructions. "Are you okay?"

She shrugged. "I'm fine. Aside from the fact that I made just about the worst possible impression at my new school."

"God, Gretchie, that's the least of it."

"I know." She sipped her tea.

"Well . . . everyone knows who you are now, I guess."

"Not the kind of fame I want."

He huffed in irritation. "Your sleeve caught on fire. Who cares what they think? Besides, I'm sure they'll all forget about it in a week."

She knew her dad was right. Still, these people were—in theory—her future friends. Things were lonely enough for her out in Walfang. She didn't want to become a pariah.

The same thought seemed to cross Johnny's mind. "So, how did you like the school?"

Gretchen gave him a half smile. "My chem teacher seemed good." She preferred strict, no-nonsense teachers. "Oh, and I met the nurse. She gave me something else to give to you." Gretchen picked up her backpack, which she had dropped at her feet. "My medical form is incomplete," she said as she pulled it out.

Johnny frowned at the form. "I already talked to the office about this," he snapped. "They were supposed to take care of it."

Gretchen lifted her eyebrows, and Johnny blew out an exasperated sigh. "I can't fill out this form, sweetie. We don't know anything about your birth mother's medical history."

Gretchen nodded. She looked down at the coffee table and reached for her mug. The truth was, she never really thought about the fact that she was adopted. She wasn't the kind of person who daydreamed about her biological mother. But now that the question was put before her, she wondered why she didn't wonder. "Do we know anything about her?"

Johnny pressed his lips together. "Just her name," he admitted.

Silence hung in the air. Gretchen took another sip of tea, waiting.

"What is it?" she asked finally.

Johnny rubbed his sideburn again. "Saskia Robicheck."

Saskia. Something about the syllables struck a chord with Gretchen, and she wondered if she had heard them before. Perhaps one of her parents had mentioned it? It seemed familiar. "With a name like that, you'd think it would be pretty easy to get information."

"You'd think," Johnny agreed with a wry smile. "But it isn't." He looked down at the form. "Well, anyway, I'll take care of this."

Gretchen sipped her tea.

"What do you want for dinner?"

"I think I'll just catch something at the diner," Gretchen said. "I've got a shift later."

Johnny looked horrified. "You're not going to work."

"Why not? I'm not hurt."

"All right." He still looked hesitant. "I don't really know how I could stop you, anyway."

"You can't."

Johnny pursed his lips and looked down at the form. Then he stood up and took Gretchen's empty tea mug.

She sat listening as his footsteps retreated to the kitchen, as the mug clinked in the sink, as his footfalls proceeded down the hall toward his studio. In a way it was a relief. *I need some alone time before work,* Gretchen thought. *I need to relax a little.*

The sound of the howling wind as she crossed over the bridge filled her ears, and a chill ran down her scalp, as if someone had just touched her hair. Gretchen turned, expecting her father, but no one was there.

She sighed and settled back onto the soft couch cushions. Outside, the leaves dripped morosely, as if they couldn't forget the storm that had passed by. Wet leaves stuck to the wood porch, slick and dreary. Fall always cast a pall of gloom over Gretchen. She never minded the frigid bite of winter. But even the hint of damp chill that came with early fall weather made her tired.

"Gretchen."

The voice broke into her thoughts, rousing her from a half sleep.

"Coming." She pushed aside the throw and hauled herself off the couch. She padded down the hall in thick woolen socks toward Johnny's studio, then knocked softly on the door, but there was no answer. She pushed it slightly ajar. Johnny was peering at his computer, his ears devoured by mammoth headphones.

Gretchen waved a little to capture his attention.

He lifted his eyebrows at her and took off the headphones. "Hey," he said.

"Hey."

They stared at each other a moment.

"You were calling me?" Gretchen prompted.

Johnny shook his head. "Sorry."

"Oh. I thought I heard—" It had been so clear. Her name. "Never mind."

Johnny frowned at her. "Why don't you take a nap, sweetie?"

Gretchen nodded. "Yeah," she said, a feeling of discomfort growing in her chest. "Maybe I will."

Chapter Six

*Will and Tim sat at the edge of the dock,
their feet dangling a foot over the water.
Will leaned forward to peer at himself,
and Tim put a hand on his chest. "Don't
fall in," he said.*

    *Will looked down at the water. It
wasn't deep; maybe three feet. He could
see a blue crab scuttling sideways along
the bottom, leaving a ragged trail in the
silt. Will turned to say something, and
his brother plunged forward. The water
splashed, covering him. And when Will
stood to look, he saw that the bottom
hadn't been the bottom after all. The
bottom was just an illusion, and now it
had vanished—Tim had disappeared
into a black void. He had stopped Will
from falling moments before the dark
water swallowed him up. . . .*

Even though they'd had an argument at lunch the day
before, Gretchen still stopped by Will's house before
school, and he still climbed into the Gremlin beside
her. Her long fingers clasped the gearshift, and he noticed the blue vein visible beneath her tanned skin on
the back of her hand. He wanted to reach out and
trace the vein with a fingertip, or sweep the loose hair
behind her ear. Any excuse to touch her would have
made him feel better, he thought. He just wanted to be

assured of her presence, her realness. But instead, what he said was, "I'm sorry."

Gretchen sighed and started up the car. "I know," she said as she backed out of the driveway.

The day was bright and clear, although there were still puddles along the edge of the road and a stiff breeze was blowing from the east. Gretchen didn't seem so nervous going over the bridge this morning, and Will sat back in his seat, relaxing, as she turned into the rear parking lot and pulled into a spot right beside a white SUV. Jefferson Lang was just stepping out, and he smiled when he saw Gretchen. He smiled the smile that had slain a thousand hearts, and said, "Hey, fireball."

Gretchen smiled back at him, and Will frowned as she said, "Hey."

Jefferson barely nodded at Will. Instead, he leaned against his car door and gave Gretchen an up-and-down look that irritated Will. "So, I wanted to let you know that I'm having a party this weekend," Jefferson said. "You should come."

"Oh." Gretchen sounded surprised. "Okay."

Jefferson gave Will a fleeting glance and added, "Bring a friend," in a way that made Will grit his teeth. He suppressed the urge to call out, "Sounds like fun, Lang, thanks for the invite!" Will was never the master of sarcasm, and he knew that it would have sounded ridiculous.

"I didn't know you knew Jefferson Lang," Will said as they headed toward the school building, and immediately wanted to kick himself.

Gretchen gave him a sidelong look. "You don't want me to talk to him, either?"

Will sighed. "No—I just . . . I just didn't know you knew him."

"He's in my chem class. I know he's good at passing out papers; that's about it."

"Right."

Will touched her elbow as they walked toward the rear doors, and at first he wasn't sure that was the right move, but she didn't shake it off.

"So, are we going to the party?" Will asked.

She stopped in her tracks and lifted her eyebrows at him. "You want to go to the party?"

He released her elbow. "Sure, why not?"

"*You* want to go to the party. You."

"Sounds like fun," Will lied. He hated parties, and he knew that Gretchen knew it. But he just didn't want to let her out of his sight. Particularly not to go hang out with Jefferson Lang.

She stared at him for a moment, as if she were trying to read his mind, and Will felt his face flush hot. He wasn't a big blusher, but he knew he was blushing now. Still, there wasn't anything he could do to stop it.

Gretchen opened her lips to say something, and Will heard, as if from far off, a shout. Then another shout, and a scream, and when he turned, Will saw a large yellow dog streaking across the wide green lawn. It was racing toward the school, coming right at Gretchen. It was barking madly, a leash dangling uselessly behind.

Will felt a flash of confusion, then fear, as he heard the dog snarl. Gretchen cried out and he heard himself scream as the dog leaped at her, slamming full force into her body and knocking her to the ground.

Chapter Seven

Hell is found at the bottom of the sea.
—Sailors' proverb

Gretchen was aware of someone screaming, but the noise was far off, almost dreamlike. Pain racked her arm. She had thrown her hands up to protect her face, and the yellow Labrador sank its teeth into the first thing it encountered. She hit at its muzzle with her other hand, but the dog had latched on and clearly had no intention of letting go.

Her jacket was of thick denim, which meant that the dog held her in a crushing vise instead of piercing her skin. An elbow to the head did not even manage to dislodge the dog's teeth. She grunted with effort as she tried to roll over on top of the dog, but it writhed away, shifting everything but its grip. It held on with the tenacity of a lunatic. It was seventy pounds of lupine sinew with madness burning in its golden eyes.

Golden eyes.

There was something about those eyes that struck her as human, and familiar, but she didn't have time to think, only to react. Heat rose in her, burned through her body. Her right arm was limp, broken perhaps, but she felt a surge of strength. She reached over with her left arm and ripped the dog from her body. Gretchen managed to fling the dog from her and leap to her feet. A canine snarl, bared teeth, a body tensed to spring—but a moment passed and Will shot forward.

"No!" Gretchen screamed as the dog lunged at him. She thrust her body between the dog and Will. Will stumbled to the ground as Gretchen landed on top of the dog, which still writhed and snarled, even pinned under her weight. Gretchen held on, ignoring the throbbing in her arm, tensing all of her concentration on subduing the dog. It was then that she became aware of a woman in a colorful sweater screaming, "Coco! Coco!" and Gretchen managed to register the irony that this ferocious beast descended from wolves had such a ridiculous name.

Someone must have called 911, because a police cruiser pulled up. The woman's pitch rose and her scream turned hoarse as an officer darted out, gun drawn.

"Shut up!" the officer shouted, but the screamer didn't shut up.

"You can't shoot!" Will shouted, and stood in front of Gretchen. The officer growled at him, but Gretchen was splayed across the dog, and Will was right—the officer couldn't have taken a shot.

The other officer was running, shouting into her radio, as the dog flailed in a final, violent motion to free itself. "Get the Taser!" she shouted.

Gretchen hesitated a moment—an image of Guernsey tore through her mind, half paralyzing her with pity—but she flattened her arm across the dog's neck.

It barked, an earsplitting challenge, and its golden eyes glittered with hate. And then suddenly the dog went limp.

Not with death, but with surrender.

Gretchen's body was stiff with tension for a moment, then—degree by degree—began to relax. Finally she released her arm from the dog's neck. Coco looked at her with big eyes and whimpered, then licked her hand.

"Don't," Will warned, but Gretchen had already rolled away, removing her weight and strength from the dog, who lay there for a moment, then struggled to its feet and shook itself.

"Coco!" The woman was crying, smearing mascara all over her puffy face as she grabbed the bright purple leash attached to Coco's collar. "Why? Why did you do that? I'm so sorry," she blubbered to Gretchen. "She's never done anything like that before."

"It's okay," Gretchen said.

"She's always been such a good dog." The woman rubbed Coco's side. The dog shook herself uncertainly again, and her tail gave a half wag.

The officers stood by, hesitating, and Gretchen noticed how young the one with the gun was. "Would you like to file a report?" the other one asked.

"Definitely," Will said.

"No," Gretchen said.

"Which is it?" the young officer snapped.

Will and Gretchen stared at each other. Will's denim-blue eyes were hard for a moment, then softened. "It's up to you," he said.

Gretchen turned to the female officer. "No, thank you."

"This dog should be reported to animal control," the officer replied.

Coco's owner wrapped her dog in a protective hug, and Gretchen suddenly felt her arm throb with pain. Tears sprang to her eyes, and her knees felt gelatinous, as if the muscles holding up her legs had melted away.

"She's a good dog," Coco's owner whimpered, on her knees beside the dog.

Gretchen blinked away her tears and swallowed a few times, hoping her voice would return. When it did, it was an uncertain croak. "It isn't the dog's fault."

"Were you teasing it?" The young officer had red hair and a spray of freckles across his nose, which—frankly—made him hard to take seriously.

Maybe that's why he has to sound like such a tool, Gretchen thought. *To make up for his innocent looks.* "I didn't do anything," she said, but her voice lacked conviction. She *hadn't* done anything, she knew that, but somehow she couldn't shake the feeling that she was somehow responsible—that the dog never would have gone crazy and attacked anyone else. The dog's eyes were brown now, but when it had attacked, they had glittered like gold. They had worn a human expression, full of power, full of hate.

Like the eyes she had seen in the waterspout.

When Gretchen looked up, she saw a group of students clustered behind the glass doors, watching the scene. Her body felt limp, her head light. Will wrapped a supporting arm around her shoulders.

"Let's get you to the doctor," he said. "I think someone should take a look at that arm."

The young officer looked like he was about to protest, but his partner said, "Let's go," in a voice that gave no options. "You'll have to make a statement," she said to Gretchen.

"Can she come to the police station later?" Will asked. "I think we should get her to the hospital right now." He didn't wait for a response, just led Gretchen away by the elbow.

Gretchen and Will started up the walkway that led around the school, avoiding bringing the spectacle inside through the double doors. Gretchen had never been so grateful for someone else's presence. She was grateful, too, for Will's silence, his refusal to get hysterical even when she felt like she was falling apart. Like *everything* was falling apart.

Behind her, Gretchen heard Coco's owner sobbing softly into the dog's yellow fur.

It's not the dog's fault. She knew it.

But she couldn't make sense of it. It was almost as if with every step she took toward answers, they receded, slipping back into the vast, mysterious ocean beyond.

No trauma.

That was what the emergency room doctor had said. "There is no trauma to your arm." She was

African, and her enunciation was rounded and musi-
cal, making the absence of trauma sound like a cele-
bration. But Gretchen didn't feel like celebrating. In
fact, she didn't even agree that there was no trauma.
True, her arm hadn't been chewed off. Thanks to the
thick material of her jacket, there weren't even any
bite marks, no blood to deal with. But there was heavy
bruising—her muscles felt as if they had been placed
under a potato masher and pulverized.

More than that, though, she felt cracked open, like
a pumpkin cut in half, oozing pulp. The bright lights
and beeping machines in the hospital, the man who
lay on a stretcher in the corner, ignored and moaning
with every exhalation, all made her want to scream.
Will's presence was the only thing that gave her comfort. And even when the doctor discharged her with a
sheaf of paperwork and let them walk back into the
day as if nothing had happened, the brilliant sunlight
seemed overwhelming.

Will took her hand and gently led her to the Gremlin. "Let me?" he asked as he pulled the keys to her car
from his pocket. She nodded; she was still in no shape
to drive. He opened the door for her and she climbed
into the passenger side. Then he held her hand as he
started for home, driving slowly, carefully, with only
his left hand on the steering wheel.

The day had grown pleasantly warm, and Gretchen
used the crank to roll down the window. She liked the
low-tech certainty of the crank. It felt good to do something under her own power, even though it was a small
thing and made her arm ache. She breathed in the

autumn smell of damp leaves, felt the cool air on her face. Gretchen and her father had often come out to their country house on weekends throughout the fall and even into the winter, so the landscape wasn't unfamiliar. But she found herself longing for the deep canyons of Manhattan, the cliffs of buildings reaching to the sky, leaving only a small strip of blue overhead. She missed the masses of people.

What am I doing here, she wondered, *underneath this wide sky?*

She felt a hot tear slip from her bottom lashes and slide silently down her cheek. She made no noise, but Will tightened his grip on her hand. He guided the car into Gretchen's driveway, the wheels crunching over the gravel as the Gremlin rolled to a stop. When he turned off the engine, silence fell, soft as snow, over them.

Will looked at her then, tucked a stray lock of hair behind her ear. "Are you all right?" he asked. He erased the track of the tear with his thumb but made no mention of it.

Gretchen felt her lips tremble. There were many things she wanted to say, but all she managed was, "Why?"

That was it. *Why? Why did Tim have to die? Why was Asia killed? Why do frightening things keep happening?*

Why can't things go back to the way they were?

Will sat back in his seat. "I don't know," he said finally. "I guess I've . . . I've just stopped asking that. It doesn't really help."

Gretchen laughed, soft and sad. "No, it doesn't."

"There's a lot of tragedies in the world, you know? Why do some kids get cancer? Why do some people live in Rwanda and get their arms chopped off?" He shrugged. "I don't know. They just do. And those people just have to figure out how to go on."

Gretchen nodded. "I just wish I knew what was happening."

"Me too."

The silence sat before them, like a smooth pool. Neither wanted to disturb it. Finally, after a long while, Will said, "You're stronger than you realize."

"I don't want to be strong. I just want . . . to take a nap." She laughed at how pathetic that sounded.

"Yeah." Will turned to her. "Well, maybe you can do that."

She closed her eyes, and he pulled her close to him. She felt the warmth of his skin through his blue and gray plaid flannel shirt, and it seemed to flow into her. Gretchen kissed his neck softly, and he pulled away in surprise.

She felt her face turn hot as he looked at her for a long moment. "I—I'm sorry," she stammered, "I didn't mean—"

He leaned forward then and pressed his lips against hers.

It was a sweet kiss, and Gretchen would forever remember the softness of his lips, the feel of his arms pressing her against his body. Happiness coursed through her like a new heartbeat.

When he pulled away, he touched her hair gently.

He smiled at her, eyes shining, and she felt then as if she might fly away, float through the window and up to the clouds. It was what she had wanted for so long, and now she had it, and it was almost too much.

She pressed her forehead against his chest, and he stroked her hair. Finally, he put his hands to her face and tilted her eyes toward his. "What was that for?" she asked, an echo of the question she had asked the last time he kissed her, innocently, in the hospital.

"For you," Will replied, his eyes serious.

Gretchen looked up at him and touched with light fingers the long scar that ran across his face. "I'm glad."

"Me too."

The car was filled with the things unsaid between them, and Gretchen felt vaguely that they should be expressed, that expectations should be explained, but in the end she was just too tired, and when Will leaned forward to kiss her again, she surrendered herself to him completely.

Chapter Eight

From the Walfang Gazette
Inspectors Find Fault in Local Bridge

High winds have been taking a toll on the Highlands Street Bridge, local authorities reported. "It's a lucky thing this bridge was due for inspection," said civil engineer Peter Hawles. "We've got a lot of high school kids taking that route every day."

It seems that high winds and extreme weather have been weakening the joists that hold the bridge together. "With the wrong set of circumstances," Hawles said, "we could have had a catastrophe on our hands."

Repair work is scheduled to take place over the weekend.

"Well, this sure is a fun outing," Carl said as he steered the battered old truck through the streets. It was drizzling lightly, but the sky was dark gray. A storm was coming.

"Thanks for taking me downtown," Gretchen said.

"Nothing better than a field trip to the police station," Carl replied. "I hope you two are scared straight!" He let out a belly laugh that filled up the car and even made Gretchen giggle a little. Will shook his head. He was wedged in the middle, between Gretchen and his uncle.

Gretchen had to make an official statement about the dog attack, so she was headed downtown to talk to Police Chief Barry McFarlan, Angus's uncle. And Will had to straighten out the beach permit mess he had created.

Unsurprisingly, his father had hit the roof when he'd heard.

"You're causing a real headache for your uncle!" Mr. Archer had screamed. "This could be a *major* problem, Will."

Will had tried to hide his irritation. Lately it seemed as if everything he did was wrong. He wished his father were a little less judgmental. "I'm sorry."

"I don't care about that," Mr. Archer snapped. "Just straighten it out."

So that's what he was doing.

Carl, on the other hand, hadn't seemed perturbed at all. He had been very understanding, and had even teased Will for getting a ticket, calling him "Mr. Safe Driver." Now he was whistling as he steered with one hand, the other arm propped on the open window frame.

Carl pulled right into a spot in front of the station and put two quarters in the meter. "Crime doesn't pay," he said to Will with a wink. Then they all walked up the concrete steps.

The Walfang police station was an old building with computers that looked as if they had been unearthed in an archeological dig. The entire police force was about fifteen people, but there were only five on duty now. The officer behind the desk pointed out the

police chief's office to Gretchen. Gretchen gave Will a
pat on the arm and started down the hall.

"Want me to come with you?" Will asked.

Gretchen didn't break her stride as she took two
backward steps, smiling at him and shaking her head.
"I can handle it, Will." She turned back and disappeared into an office. Will bit his lip, wondering what
she would say. The way she had insisted that it wasn't
the dog's fault had unnerved him. What had she
meant by that?

"How can I help you?" The officer, a young Latina
with a professional air, lifted her eyebrows at Carl.

"We're just here to take care of this parking ticket."
Carl handed over the orange slip.

"I was borrowing his truck," Will explained. "We
don't want it to go on my uncle's record."

"Just a minute." The officer—Tejada, her name tag
read—typed some numbers into the computer, then
waited. She smiled at them apologetically. "Slow," she
explained.

"Take your time," Carl said, leaning against the re-
ception desk.

A soft insect-like sound hummed in Will's ears. He
didn't pay much attention until he noticed his uncle's
head snap up.

Will watched as Carl turned. There was a holding
cell a few feet away, up the hall in the opposite direction from which Gretchen had gone. A figure sat,
hunched in the corner, unmoving.

Will heard the sound again. It was a long, sing-
song note.

Horror flashed across Will's uncle's face as the figure slowly, slowly lifted his head. Will didn't know the man, but the look in his eyes was terrifying as he sang on.

"Hey, shut up," Officer Tejada snapped.

Will grabbed his uncle's elbow. "Are you okay?"

Carl's eyes were wide, and for a moment he stared at Will as if he had no idea who he was. Then he blinked. "I think . . . can you handle this, Will?" Carl gestured to Officer Tejada. "I need some air."

"Do you know that guy?" Will asked. Will looked over at the man. Pockmarked face, flashing eyes—it wasn't anyone he'd seen before.

"No." Carl's voice was a whisper as he stepped past Will.

Will stared, and the man stared back. A smile slithered across his face, twisting like the branch of a poison tree. His eyes gleamed golden and then, suddenly, the fire in them disappeared. It was as if he had been lit by a momentary spark that had flared and then died out.

"Okay," Officer Tejada said at last, frowning at the computer screen. "As long as this is paid off, there shouldn't be a problem with your uncle's record. Are you prepared to pay it now?" She looked up at Will with dark eyes.

It took a long moment for her words to fall into place, and for Will to find the meaning in them. "Yes," he said at last. "Yes, I can pay it." He cast a furtive glance at the man in the holding cell, but he had turned back to the wall.

Will took care of the ticket, then waited for Gretchen in the hallway. When she came out of Barry's office, Will hurried to her side.

"Ugh. That was painful," Gretchen said. "Everything taken care of at your end?"

"Yeah." Will held her arm gently, making sure to guide her as far away from the holding cell as possible. But there was no sound from the suspect. Will cast a glance over his shoulder as they walked toward the front door. The rain had picked up, and the fat drops hit them as they hurried to the truck.

Carl was waiting for them, seated behind the wheel.

"Thanks again, Carl," Gretchen said as she climbed inside after Will. "That wasn't fun; I'm glad I had some company."

Carl didn't reply—he just nodded as he turned the key in the ignition and brought the truck to life. The blood seemed to have drained out of him.

"Let's get out of here," Will said. They pulled away from the curb, and he watched the police station in the rearview mirror until it was out of sight.

The scene at the station had disquieted him, and now—hours later—he replayed the scene with the dog in an endless loop in his mind. Over and over, he saw the flash of bared teeth, the tense muscles spring forward; he felt his heart drop as the Lab knocked Gretchen to the ground. He'd been consumed by fear, rage and fear, and in the fury that consumed him, he would have killed the animal.

He had seen the dog, seen it attack, but it had reminded Will of a sailboat, invisible wind driving it forward. What had made it go momentarily mad? He looked out his window at the house across the creek. The sky was darkening into gray twilight and Gretchen's room cast a yellow glow onto the almost-changing leaves of the maple tree that framed her window. She wasn't in her room, but Will was comforted that he was able to watch her home from his perch on his bed. She was inside the old farmhouse, safe.

He looked down at the flute in his hand. It was lightweight, made of human bone, and the length of his forearm. A sense of foreboding fell over him.

The kiss that afternoon had taken him by storm, but not by surprise. He wondered why they hadn't done it before. The moment he felt her gentle, hesitant lips against his neck, Will knew that a pass had been reached, and now there was no going back. The kiss he gave her was like a dam opening, unleashing a torrent of pent-up emotion. He could no longer deny that he loved Gretchen with a ferocity that frightened him. The touch of her skin, the sweet smell of her hair— these things were precious to him, and when he'd kissed her again, he hadn't wanted to let her go. His desire to protect her had only grown more desperate. Love had bound them together and ignited a flickering, warming light within the wreckage of his ruined life.

He hadn't wanted to leave her, but Gretchen felt she had to explain about the dog attack to her father, and she wanted to do it alone. So he had kissed her again on the doorstep, feeling the heat of her body pressed against his, and had finally let her go.

Then he'd made his way back to his house.

His mother had been in the kitchen, relaxing with a cup of coffee, when he got back from the police station. She looked up at Will and smiled. It was the kind of smile that he hadn't seen from her for a long time, as though all of her worries had vanished and she was just happy to see him. Impulsively Will had stepped behind her and kissed the top of her head. She took the hand he had rested on her shoulder and squinted up at his face. "What's wrong?" she had asked, but her voice was surprised, not worried.

"Nothing," Will had whispered, squeezing her soft hand.

She'd looked down at her coffee cup. "Dinner's at six."

"Dinner's always at six."

He'd taken the stairs up to his room and thrown his book bag on the floor. He stepped over to the window and looked out, over at Gretchen's house. He saw her brush past the window. Then she moved toward the door and disappeared.

He'd turned back to his bureau, and a shiver had rippled through his body. Sitting atop the polished dark wood was a flute that Barry McFarlan had given him. It had been found on board the *Vagabond* after the accident, and Barry had assumed it belonged to Tim. Will later discovered that it was a flute that the Sirens used to call to one another. Asia had told him that.

He usually kept it buried in his bottom drawer. He had no idea how it had appeared on top of his bureau. Reaching out, he'd touched the smooth bone with a tentative finger. Then he lifted the flute in his hands, weighing the delicate heft of it.

I must have put it there, he mused now. *I must have put it there and forgotten.*

It was a reasonable thought. Unlikely . . . but more reasonable than the alternative, which was that someone had broken into his room and placed the flute on the bureau for him to find. Although even that wasn't out of the realm of possibility. His first thought was of Kirk.

But why would he do that?

God, who can explain anything that kid does? Will argued with himself.

Kirk had stolen the flute once before and used it to call the Sirens. Will wondered if Kirk had done that again, and an ugly feeling of dread crept over him. *But the seekriegers are dead,* he reasoned. *I saw them die in the fire on the bay.*

Still, Will didn't like what the presence of the flute might mean. He thought back to the word that had been scrawled on his mirror—*FURY.* He'd written it off as a trick of the imagination. But the flute wasn't imaginary. And the dog was definitely not imaginary.

Little by little, the drops were collecting into a pool. Will had a bad feeling that something evil was on the rise. Something connected with Gretchen.

So he sat down on his bed and watched her house. It looked the same as usual. Will didn't know what he had expected—a dark cloud, an evil presence. It was just an old farmhouse, the porch flecked with falling leaves, a few yellow mums blooming in the front flower-bed. The house comforted him with its sense of usual-ness.

That was why he stayed there, on the bed, watch-ing the house for the next hour. And it was why he came back to his perch after dinner and watched until darkness fell and the moon rose. He watched until Gretchen's light went out and the night was broken only by a lamp on the first floor—a sign that Johnny was still awake, working on a song.

Will watched, unsure of what he was watching for. He watched the house beneath the cold, beautiful stars and wouldn't tear his eyes away, not even to sleep.

He stayed that way for a long time. Finally he re-membered that he had some reading to do for school. He dug out the novel and scanned the first page, look-ing up after every paragraph to check on Gretchen's house. This half-captured attention made it hard to focus on the text in front of him. The letters didn't want to add up to words. The more he tried to focus, the more their meaning dissolved before him. Even when he took a single word, *agile*. Was that even a word? *Ag. Ile. A. Gile. Agi. Le.* He looked at it, and looked at it, until the alphabet fell apart for him, useless.

Will tossed the book onto his bed and looked out the window, watching the light from Johnny's window as it lingered, golden, on the small mound of yellow maple leaves beneath the tree outside Gretchen's win-dow. It was an unfinished pile, one that Johnny must have started and left in a moment of distraction. It wasn't hard to remember jumping in a pile like that. Playing with Tim, Guernsey barking madly and rolling onto her back, sending yellow leaves into the air with her wild limbs. Will touched the edge of his ancient quilt, missing his dog with a persistent ache. Guernsey had been thirteen when she died. Will and Tim had gotten her as a puppy when Will was five. Almost all of the life he could remember had Guernsey in it.

He remembered picking her out when she was a wiggly puppy, graceless and curious. A friend's dog had had puppies, and Tim was in charge of choosing the one they took home. Will got to pick the name. Somehow, it was as if naming the dog had bound Guernsey to Will permanently, and she was his dog ever after that. She slept on his bed and followed him through the house. Tim would complain, but even when he scooped up the sleeping puppy and put her on his own bed, she would eventually wake up, hop off, and clamber onto Will's bed again.

A soft tinkle, like ice fracturing, broke into Will's thoughts. Then a crash. *Raccoons are into something,* Will thought, but then he heard a muttered curse. Will looked out the window. A familiar shape was huddled beneath the tree. The shape groaned, then started to sing softly.

> *There's no sign of canvas on the blue waves,*
> *You'll never return home to me.*

For the waves beat the shore like a
  knock at the door,
And all things return to the sea. . . .

Will's heart gave a sickening lurch, the tune awak-
ening half-remembered images in his mind. Asia's
green, haunting eyes. Kirk's voice. Yes, Will had heard
this song before. Kirk had sung it once. Will had been
with Asia then, and they had listened to the mournful
tune, sweet and piercing as grief.

But this wasn't Kirk's voice. It was a deep, rum-
bling bass. A familiar, bearlike growl.

He bolted down the hall, his heart hammering. His
mother didn't look up from the television screen as he
passed her room, then hurried down the stairs. Out
the back door, out into the yard.

The man looked up at him but didn't speak.

"Uncle Carl?" Will said gently.

Carl peered at him with bleary eyes. "Dropped my
bottle," he said.

Shattered glass shimmered across the flagstones.
The label was facedown, the only thing holding together several shards of glass cut by a spiderweb of
cracks. But Will didn't need to see the label to know
what the bottle had contained. He walked over to his
uncle and knelt beside him. "Are you okay?" he asked.

Carl held up a hand. A bloody cut ran across his
palm. "Tried to pick up some of the pieces."

"We'll have to get this cleaned up." Will's brain
burned with ideas—ways he could get Carl into the

house without his parents knowing. *Dad threw a total fit when I got a parking ticket. What will he do if he thinks Carl is drinking again?*

"I'm sorry, Will," Carl said, his words thick and slurred, as if his tongue were now a heavy sponge. "I know I've made a mess." He looked at the broken glass, his face distraught.

"It's okay," Will told his uncle, although this was a lie. It wasn't okay. It wasn't. Will hadn't seen Carl drink in years. Not even a glass of wine with Thanksgiving dinner.

"Don't tell your parents."

"I won't."

"They won't let you ride in the truck with me anymore."

Carl muttered something unintelligible, then started to sing again. Will cut him off. "What are you even doing here?" he asked as he struggled to help his uncle to his feet.

"Just checking," was the obscure answer. Carl clearly remembered that they had to be quiet—he was whispering.

Will helped him to the steps that led to the mudroom, which opened into the kitchen. From there, they could get to the downstairs bathroom without passing his parents' bedroom or his father's office.

"Checking on what?"

But Carl didn't answer.

Will trod softly on the wooden steps, but it wasn't easy when he was half dragging a two-hundred-pound man with him. He watched carefully where he put his feet, and guided Carl toward the mudroom using the outer edges of the boards, which creaked less.

But in the end, it was wasted effort. Mr. Archer was sitting at the table when they walked into the kitchen. His face was a mask of alarm as he set down the glass he had been drinking from. "You're bleeding," he said to Carl.

"He cut his hand," Will explained.

"I cut my hand," Carl repeated in his thick voice.

"You're drunk." Will's father's face betrayed no emotion—not surprise, not anger. He turned to Will, and for a moment Will feared that his father was going to accuse him of letting this happen. Instead Mr. Archer just said, "Make some coffee while I get him cleaned up. And be quiet about it. If your mother hears, we're in deep."

Will nodded and transferred Carl's bulk to his father's steady shoulder.

"I'm sorry, Bert," Carl slurred. "I don't know what happened. I was just buying some things at the store, and I don't even know what made me grab it—"

"Quiet," his brother told him.

Clearly chastened, Carl clammed up as Mr. Archer led him to the downstairs bathroom. Will opened the freezer and pulled out the ground coffee, then measured the water and set it to brew. He was more than a little surprised by his father's reaction—concern but not judgment. Will had expected his father to storm, to scream. That's what he would have done if Will had ever come home drunk . . . and Will wasn't a recovering alcoholic.

When Will was small, he would tell his mother, "I love you with my whole heart." And his mother would say, "What about Daddy?"

"I have another heart for Daddy," Will would reply, in complete ignorance of human anatomy. That response always made his mother laugh.

But maybe, somehow, everyone does have different hearts for different people, Will mused. The way his father loved Carl was different from the way he loved Will. Just as the way he loved Will was different from the way he had loved Tim.

Carl and Tim, for some reason, got a more forgiving love. The Mr. Archer they knew was different from Will's father. Different, but the same.

Pink light stole through his window, and Will woke with a start. He was half covered with a blanket and the lamp on his bedside table had been turned off, and he realized that his mother must have looked into his room on her way down to start the early-morning baking. A glance out the window showed only the unchanged house, which revealed no clue as to Gretchen's safety.

His father had taken Carl to the hospital to get stitched up. Mr. Archer had come home after two hours, looking grim. "Your uncle's going to be all right," he'd said, but Will had to wonder. *What made him take a drink in the first place?*

The adventure had left Will feeling tired and confused. He'd gone back upstairs to watch Gretchen's
house. He wasn't even sure what he was looking for,
but he'd planned to be there all night.

He tossed away the covers, and the flute tumbled
out of them. Will's heart sank. *What if Gretchen went
sleepwalking again? What if I fell asleep and missed
it? What if something . . .*

Cursing himself, he flung himself out of bed and
across the room. He dashed down the stairs and into
the kitchen, where Gretchen was sitting at the table,
drinking from a chipped white mug.

She cocked her head in calm confusion. "Pulling
an all-nighter?" she asked, nodding in the direction of
Will's rumpled clothes.

He stopped short and rubbed his face with his
hands. Then he sagged, leaning against the counter-
top. "I just—thought I was late."

"You are late." She smiled and walked over to him.
"But not hideously. I was a little early, so I decided to
come in and help myself." She tilted her face to him,
and he leaned down, tasting the coffee sweetness on
her lips.

The back door flew open, and Will looked up into
his uncle's startled face. Gretchen moved away and
took a sip of her coffee as Will scratched at his arm
and said, "Hey, Uncle Carl."

"Hey. Is your dad around?" Carl nodded at Gretchen
but skipped his usual cheerful, blustery greeting.

"He's at the farm stand," Gretchen said.

Carl nodded again.

"What happened to your hand?" Gretchen asked, indicating the white gauze that rested between his palm and the door.

"Cut it," Carl said sharply. His chin trembled, as if he wanted to add something, but he just flashed Will an unreadable look and headed out the back door.

"Pretty subdued," Gretchen said.

"Yeah." Will could think of a few reasons for that, given his drunken ramblings the night before. But what popped into his mind was Carl saying that he was "just checking." Checking on what? Will looked up and realized that she was watching him. "I'd better change my shirt."

"And put on some shoes," Gretchen agreed. "We've got to get out of here."

"Do you—do you want to come with me?" Will blushed as he asked.

"Up to your room?" Gretchen sounded wryly surprised. "Then we'll never get out of here."

"I didn't mean—" Will shook his head. All he'd meant was that he didn't want to let Gretchen out of his sight. But it did sound suggestive . . . not that he was opposed to that idea, either. "Okay." He grinned sheepishly and headed up to his room, alone.

Gretchen is fine, he told himself. *She's fine.*

But when he opened the door to his room, the flute was still on his bed.

Chapter Nine

Circe Invidiosa
John William Waterhouse, 1849–1917

Here, Waterhouse achieves brilliant narrative effect with a few telling details. *Circe Invidiosa* means "envious Circe," and in this image we see the famous sea witch dripping green poison into the water where the beautiful sea nymph, Scylla, bathes. When sea deity Glaucus confessed his love for Scylla, Circe became filled with jealousy. Her poison turned Scylla into a hideous sea monster, seen here—at the moment of change—below Circe's feet.

Mafer had asked Gretchen if they could meet at her family's apartment, which was down the street from the library in Waterbreak. Waterbreak was actually smaller than Walfang but had a tiny movie theater, a few shops, a decent Italian restaurant and an excellent Polish one, and a library.

Mafer lived in a complex of duplex apartments, brick with white trim. The grass was mowed, but a few stray tufts at the edges showed a lack of attention to detail. Every apartment revealed the character of its residents. In front of one, there were two toddler bicycles and a pink striped toy stroller. Another bore a collection of wind chimes that tinkled with crazy merriment as a breeze blew by, tickling them. A third sported a few mums in pots and a fat orange cat, watching Gretchen with calm reserve from its perch in the window.

Somehow Gretchen knew which apartment was Mafer's even before she saw the brass number beside the door. Bright yellow heliopsis grew in a tall, wild bunch, the yellow blooms falling over each other like friendly, affectionate drunks. An orange and black butterfly sat on a flower, pulsing its wings as if in concentration. Below, a riot of blue Michaelmas daisies carpeted the ground. This apartment was brilliant with color and life and seemed to hold hidden depths, just like Mafer herself.

Beside the door was a cross the size of Gretchen's hand. It was covered in small tin charms, each one unique: a pair of praying hands, a dancer, a sock. Gretchen rang the doorbell and heard it chime through the apartment. A young boy, about eight, answered the door. He had large black eyes and looked up at Gretchen with excitement. "You're Mafer's friend?" he asked, and before Gretchen could answer, he darted off.

Gretchen stepped into the living room, which was cramped despite being uncluttered. There was a tiny blue plaid love seat placed across from an ancient-looking television. A large bookcase, holding framed photos and volumes in both English and Spanish, lined one wall. Gretchen walked over to inspect a photograph of a young woman in uniform. Beside that image was one of the Virgin Mary—again, the frame overlaid with small tin trinkets.

A rustle behind her made Gretchen turn. She had expected to see Mafer, but instead a small woman with gray hair was watching her. Her face was round, her bright eyes watchful and merry.

"Hi," Gretchen said awkwardly. "I'm Gretchen."

The woman nodded.

"Are you Mafer's grandmother?"

A shrug. "Yes." Perhaps it was just her accent, but her tone of voice communicated perfectly how little she was interested in stating the obvious. It didn't hurt Gretchen's feelings, though. On the contrary, it made her want to laugh.

"Is this your daughter?" Gretchen pointed to the photograph.

"She's in Afghanistan. Third tour of duty."

"That must be hard for you."

"We are very proud of her."

"Of course."

The old woman narrowed her eyes. She looked deeply into Gretchen's face. "Y dónde está tu mama, mija?" she asked gently, but in a voice that expected no answer.

Gretchen understood a little Spanish—enough to translate the question. *And where is your mother, my dear?*

The old woman's smile chilled her. Not because it held any malice—only because it seemed to know the answer.

Just then Mafer bounded down the stairs, followed by her little brother. The noise broke the spell.

"We're just going to the library," Mafer was saying.

"Can't I come?"

"Ask a friend to come over, Joaquin," she replied. She touched his hair gently. "Or go outside and play."

"I'd rather be with you."

Gretchen wondered how Mafer could resist those big eyes, that adoring gaze.

Mafer gave Joaquin a kiss on the cheek. "I'll be back in two hours. You'll survive. Keep an eye on Abuelita."

"You come with me," Mafer's grandmother said. "We're going to make churros."

Joaquin grinned. "And we won't make any for Mafer."

"What?" Mafer screeched in mock horror. "*Malcri-ado!* Gretchen, let's get out of here. Have you met my grandmother? Abuelita, this is Gretchen."

"Yo conozco esta huérfana," Abuelita said. "La hija del fuego."

Silence pulsed through the room. Gretchen felt as if she could hear the sound of her own blood traveling through her veins.

She caught the sideways glance Mafer tried to sneak at her, and felt her friend's embarrassment.

"What does that mean?" Gretchen asked finally. "Daughter of fire—what do you mean by that?"

Mafer's grandmother smiled. "You speak Spanish." She didn't seem at all surprised, and she didn't offer any further explanation.

Mafer yanked open the door. "Okay, we've got to go," she said quickly, half shoving Gretchen out the door. When it closed behind them, Gretchen felt as if

she had just returned to the real world, leaving a confusing dream on the other side of the wall behind her.

"God—I have no idea why she just said that." Mafer
grabbed Gretchen's hand as soon as the door was
shut behind them. "I'm so sorry."

"It's okay."

"She's a little crazy, my grandmother."

Gretchen nodded, but she didn't believe what
Mafer said. The older woman's mind was so sharp it
could slice through metal. No, she wasn't crazy. Not
at all. "I'm adopted," Gretchen said.

Mafer bit her lip. "That only makes it worse."

"You knew that." Gretchen stopped and watched
her friend squirm.

Mafer pulled her fingers through the ends of her
long dark hair. It was her peculiar habit, Gretchen
had noticed. "Sometimes, Gretchen, we . . . My family.
We know things about people. We don't find out. We
don't ask. We just . . ." She lifted her shoulders, then
let them drop. "We just know. But I don't know why
my grandmother just called you an orphan. What was
she thinking?"

Gretchen couldn't fight the feeling that this was
exactly the conversation Mafer's grandmother had
wanted them to have. She had said what she did because she wanted to tell Gretchen something. And
what she wanted to tell Gretchen was this: *I know
things about you.*

It was a thought that might have frightened some
people, but not Gretchen. But it did leave her with a
feeling of unease. *What did the woman know?*

* * *

The Waterbreak library was a boxy, eighties-style modern building with an entire wall of windows. The children's section was upstairs, and the main research area was downstairs. A corpulent librarian stood behind the circulation desk, organizing DVDs on a cart. He didn't look up as the girls stepped inside, even though there was only one other person—a white-haired gentleman, reading quietly at a library table— in the whole place. The long wall of windows was tinted, and the light that crept in cast everything in sepia.

To Gretchen, the library felt like a safe place. She had often come here with her father when she was younger, as the video collection was better than the one in Walfang. In general, Gretchen preferred the Walfang library, with its small, snug spaces and nineteenth-century architecture. But Waterbreak had more resources, including a research room with an aggregating system that made article searches easy and comfortable chairs for collaborating. This was where the girls were headed now, as they passed the spinning racks of paperbacks and the cozy reading chairs gathered around a low wooden coffee table. Mafer led the way and took a seat at a wide library table. She removed her off-white jacket and slung it over the back of a chair. "Okay," she said, pulling their science text from her messenger bag. "Want to check and see if there are any articles to back up what we're saying?"

"Sure." Gretchen pulled her library card from her

wallet and walked over to the bank of computers. Gretchen typed in her card number and logged on to the system. In the moment it took for her computer to boot up, she found herself staring at a painting on the far wall. She knew the painter—John William Waterhouse. He had never been one of her favorites. Gretchen preferred contemporary art, and this painting, like many Waterhouse paintings, was an idealized, romantic image of a classical subject. A beautiful woman sat by the sea, combing her long hair. An almost serpentine tail wrapped around her, gleaming. Her lips were parted, as if she might be singing to herself.

An image of Kirk's drawing rose in her mind—the head half out of the water, the eyes peering out from the dark shadow. That was more how Gretchen imagined a mermaid. Threatening. Terrifying.

She thought of the seekriegers out on the bay. She remembered them—dimly. She remembered that they were terrifying.

This innocuous mermaid in the painting before her seemed like a lie.

Almost reflexively, Gretchen turned and looked at the wall behind her. On it was another Waterhouse reproduction. But this was no innocuous mermaid. In this painting, a woman held out a poison-green bowl in both hands, offering it to the viewer. She wore a long, toga-like wrap in peacock colors, and her bare feet stood on water. Her chin was tilted at an angle so that she was looking up, from beneath her eyelashes, in a pose that might have been coquettish, but here seemed menacing.

Gretchen found herself standing before the print, studying the face. There was something in the expression that seemed familiar, yet sent a chill through her. The small plaque below it read *Circe Invidiosa.*

"You call that research?" Mafer asked.

Gretchen nearly jumped at the voice by her elbow.

Mafer smiled at her apologetically. "Sorry. I didn't mean to scare you."

"No—I'm sorry. I just . . . got distracted."

Mafer crossed her arms across her chest, studying the painting. "Circe," she said, almost as if it were the name of someone she knew and didn't really approve of. "Not someone to mess with."

"All I remember is that she turned Odysseus's men into pigs."

"Then he had to come and save them. She kept him on that island for years." Mafer pursed her lips. "I like how it almost seems as if she's standing on some sea creature—a giant squid, or an octopus, maybe. Probably some poor guy who washed up on her shore." She leaned toward the painting and whispered, "Don't drink whatever's in that bowl!"

Gretchen tried unsuccessfully to suppress a laugh as the librarian strode in wearing a disapproving frown. He glanced at them sternly, tucked his button-down shirt into his pants, and stalked off.

"I like how his tie only comes halfway down his belly," Mafer noted as they watched him leave. "He looks like Papa Bear in my old Goldilocks book."

This made Gretchen giggle again.

Mafer poked Gretchen in the shoulder. "Okay, get

to work," she said mock-sternly. "Art appreciation hour is over."

They made their way back to their chairs, but when Gretchen sat down at the keyboard, she was suddenly overwhelmed by an urge to do something she had never done before. She wanted to look for her mother. Her biological mother.

But she didn't even know where to start. She racked her brain for clues. Hadn't Johnny mentioned that she was born in Boston? Her birth certificate was sealed. She had never seen it.

Before she knew what she was doing, she typed in "boston adoption gretchen ellis."

It was the usual search engine mess that you get when you don't know exactly what you're looking for: hundreds of entries, but nothing that seemed remotely relevant. Gretchen took a deep breath, trying to get some oxygen to her spinning head. *Why did I even do that?* She had never tried to research her mother before, and here she was in the library just doing it. With no thought. No intention.

The only answer she could come up with was that Mafer's grandmother had called her *huérfana*, "orphan." Which she supposed she was. And "fire's daughter," whatever that meant.

It unnerved her slightly that she had just tried a potentially life-altering search on a whim.

But nothing came of it, anyway.

She didn't know what she was feeling. There were traces of relief mixed with sadness and confusion.

Fire's daughter. What could it mean? Did that mean that her mother had died in a fire?

Gretchen looked down at her arm, the one that should have been burned in the lab the other day. She couldn't help feeling as if she were looking at a pointillist painting—all she could see was dots. One dot was the seekriegers that night on the bay with Will. One dot was the fire that didn't hurt her arm. One dot was that Mafer's grandmother had called her "fire's daughter." One dot was the dog attack. If only she could step backward, she'd be able to see the whole picture. The clues would add up to some clear meaning.

She felt a pair of eyes on her. Mafer gave her a lopsided smile. "Got some good articles?" she asked. Something in her tone suggested that she knew Gretchen wasn't looking at science.

"Working on it," Gretchen said.

She cleared her last entry and started a new search.

Chapter Ten

From the Walfang Gazette
Amateur Astronomers Prepare for
Meteor Shower

Tonight is prime viewing for the Orionids meteor shower, which causes a beautiful show of meteors and has been known to produce fireballs.

"It's exciting for us, as a club," said Walfang Astronomers Association president Jenna Riley. "It's a rare event, and we anticipate something amazing."

Although not as active as the Leonids, this shower often peaks at a rate of 20 meteors per hour. . . .

"Remind me why I'm doing this again," Will said as Gretchen brought the car to a stop by the side of the road and pulled it behind a long line of parked cars.

"I have no idea," Gretchen confessed.

Will laughed and took her hand. Then he kissed her wrist, right at the place below the palm where the blue veins showed through. "Tell me why you want to go to this party when you could be sitting at home watching a movie with me."

"Because I'm the weird new girl, and I want to erase that, get to know people. I don't want to spend my senior year with just two friends."

Will felt that he would happily have spent the rest

of the year with only Gretchen, but he didn't say so. He understood what she was saying . . . intellectually. Emotionally, he felt sick of most of the same faces he'd known since kindergarten, and he had a hard time understanding why Gretchen would want to spend time with them.

Still, he didn't want to send her into the party alone. He opened the door and stepped out onto the grass. Gretchen walked around the car to join him on the sidewalk, and the two of them started toward Jefferson Lang's house.

It was lit up, a tasteful white ranch house in one of the older sections of Walfang. Jefferson's father owned a security business, and they weren't sick rich, like most of the summer families. They were townie rich— wealthy enough to have an elegant little house with a large yard bordering the Mill River, but not wealthy enough for a mansion by the sea.

The backyard was strung with lemon-size Chinese lanterns. In the center of the yard was a large beech tree, and kids were gathered beneath its branches in groups of twos and threes.

A table was laid out with food—a twelve-foot-long sandwich cut into slices, platters of sliced watermelon, and chips and dip. There were two coolers overflowing with bottled drinks and ice, and a keg set up along the roots of the tree.

"Pretty," Gretchen said to herself, almost dreamily.

"I'm sure his mom did most of it," Will said, and Gretchen laughed. He smiled then, hearing how petty and jealous he sounded. Well—so what? Jefferson was tall and handsome and thought he owned the world. He had about as much depth as a kiddie pool.

"There's Mafer!" Gretchen waved, and her friend started over to say hello.

Will watched the way Mafer walked—her slow movements made her seem as if she were studying everyone at the party the way a vulture would. She seemed apart from the others but somehow interested in them, yet there was warmth in her smile as she greeted Gretchen.

"This is my friend Will," Gretchen said.

"Hello."

Mafer nodded at him. "Hi."

"Looks like Jefferson invited the entire school."

"I'm sure he didn't need to," Mafer said. "He invited three people, and they invited everyone else."

"Speak of the devil," Will said. Here he was now, waving at Gretchen and jogging over to say hello. Will touched Gretchen's elbow in a possessive gesture and immediately felt an odd mix of embarrassment at his behavior and pride in being there with Gretchen.

"Gretchen, you made it!" Jefferson beamed, flashing those even white teeth. He nodded at Will. "Hey, man, surprised to see you here."

"I can never resist a hero sandwich," Will said, and Gretchen narrowed her eyes at him.

"Looks like half the school is in your backyard." Gretchen gestured at the crowd beneath the tree. "We had to park a full block away."

"That's *good*! People need a party, am I right?"

Gretchen agreed, but Will didn't hazard an answer. He could hardly guess at what people needed.

"Hey, come on down to the river, I want to show you something," Jefferson said, taking Gretchen by the elbow.

Will looked at Mafer, but she just lifted her eyebrows and waved at him with her fingers as Will was forced to relinquish his hold on Gretchen. He trailed along behind as Jefferson led Gretchen down a steep slope to the river. The air was cool and clear as they crossed the grass. Near the water was a rack, and something covered by a blue tarp. Jefferson pulled it away, showing a beautiful wooden canoe. The athlete gave the dark wood a paternal smile and looked up at Gretchen. "I made it. Isn't she a beauty?"

"Oh, yes," Gretchen whispered as she touched the boat.

Will wanted to agree, but he was too surprised— and annoyed. Who would have guessed that Jefferson held secret depths of passion and talent?

"I worked on her all summer—just finished up last week." He looked over at Gretchen and asked, almost shyly, "Maybe you'd like to take her out on the river with me sometime."

Gretchen hesitated, and Will said, "Gretchen doesn't like water."

Jefferson looked at him, surprised. "Really?"

A flash of annoyance crossed Gretchen's face, but she didn't contradict him. Will winced a little, realizing that she must have thought he was trying to pick her friends for her again. Which he wasn't. Well, not intentionally.

"Hey, what are we doing down here?" called a voice, and Angus loped down the hill with his awkward, long-legged stride. "Nice boat! Should we go fishing?"

"Jefferson made the boat," Will said, feeling that he had to make nice now.

"Really? You're a man of many talents." Angus looked impressed. "Um, listen, I hate to bug you, but you're out of chips, and Kirk Worstler is up in your tree."

"What?" Jefferson tied the tarp back into place.

"You can just tell me where the chips are," Angus volunteered.

"I'm more worried about the lunatic in my tree," Jefferson said.

"He's not a lunatic," Gretchen put in, but Jefferson didn't respond.

"We'd better go see if he's okay," Will said, knowing better than to get into an argument about Kirk.

"He's not doing anything," Angus insisted as they all started up the slope. "He's just sitting there."

The crowd cleared a bit as Jefferson strode to the tree and looked up. "I don't see him." He squinted into the leaves.

"He's there." This was from Mafer. "Near the top." She didn't look up, just took another sip of her soda.

"I can't see him," Jefferson repeated.

Mafer shrugged. "Listen."

They did, then, but Will couldn't hear anything. "What is it?" he whispered to Gretchen.

"Singing," she replied, and from the expression on her face, Will could tell that the music had an eerie quality that unnerved her.

"Hey, it's not a party until Kirk does something weird, right?" Angus pronounced.

"Kirk!" Jefferson shouted. "Kirk, get down from there!"

Nothing happened for a moment; then the leaves rustled and Kirk dropped to a lower branch. He hung for a moment and jumped in front of Jefferson. Kirk looked up at the football player, who was almost a head taller than he was.

People had stopped to stare, but Kirk's expression was innocent. "What's wrong?"

"You were up in my tree!" Jefferson exclaimed. "What if you broke your neck? You're on my property— my family is liable."

"I just wanted a view."

"Of what?" Jefferson demanded.

"The meteor shower," Kirk explained. "There's supposed to be one tonight." He gazed helplessly at Gretchen. "Isn't there?"

"What?" She shook her head, clearly confused, and Will didn't know whether to throttle Kirk or offer to take him home. God, why did he have to be so weird? Still, Will got the sense that Kirk really was trying to be normal—that the poor spaced-out kid didn't have any idea that most people don't climb trees at a keg party.

A ripple of surprise ran through the crowd, and when Will looked up, he saw silver rain falling from the black night sky. Like shimmering fireworks, the translucent tails drifted across the darkness as the brilliant heads descended toward the horizon.

"It looks like the stars are falling into the river," Angus said, and Will was shocked that his friend had managed to capture the poetic essence of what was happening. It did look as if the stars were falling into the river, and the water reflected their light, rippling and dancing like silver flames.

"Fire on the water," Kirk whispered, and Will saw Gretchen shudder.

The shower didn't last long—not more than twenty seconds—and when it was over, the partygoers burst into applause, as if Jefferson had planned the spectacle for their entertainment. Then the chatter began again, this time at increased volume.

Kirk looked at Gretchen then, his large eyes resting on her with an unreadable expression.

"What is it?" she asked.

"It's nothing," Will said, before Kirk could answer.

"Wow!" Angus said. "Wow! That was awesome!" He clapped Kirk on the shoulder and said, "Aren't you sorry you weren't up in that tree?"

Kirk looked at him, then turned away, letting Angus's hand drop from his shoulder.

Angus opened his mouth, as if he might call Kirk back, but Gretchen touched his arm. "Don't," she said.

Angus looked at her serious face. "Okay," he said.

"You don't look so good," Mafer told her, and Gretchen squeezed her eyes shut.

"I have a headache," she admitted.

"Let's get out of here," Will suggested.

"Okay," Gretchen said faintly. She let him drag her away, much to his relief.

They climbed into the Gremlin, and Gretchen sat behind the wheel. It was quiet, and the noise from the party provided a low murmuring background to the darkness that surrounded them.

Gretchen put her hands to her face.

"Are you okay?" Will asked, touching her shoulder, and she leaned into him. She was crying, softly, making no sound, just the gentle, shaky intake of breath. "Hey," Will said. "Hey." And he wrapped his arms around her.

"Fire on the water," Gretchen whispered.

"I know."

"I remember it. The night on the bay."

Will felt deafened by his own heart. "You do?"

Gretchen shook her head, her eyes closed against his chest. "Just now. I'd forgotten—but now I remember."

"What else?" His voice was a whisper, faint and strange to his own ears.

"I remember those things."

"The seekriegers. Sirens."

"And . . . Asia was there. Wasn't she?"

Will couldn't speak. He nodded.

"And they all died. They died in the fire."

Will nodded again, still mute.

"But—" She looked up at him with those limpid blue eyes. "Why was Asia there? Was she one of them?"

Her face was a shifting kaleidoscope of confusion, fear, pain.

"No," Will said.

"How do you know?"

"She told me."

"But—why was she there?"

"She was . . ." Will's tongue felt heavy. He wasn't sure what to say. "She was trying to protect you."

Gretchen watched his face carefully. "But she was *something.*"

"She was a Siren," Will admitted. "But she wasn't one of them."

"She died because of me."

"It isn't your fault." He pulled her to him, trying not to remember the blood-red eyes, the monster Gretchen had become when she lit the surface of the bay with fire. *That wasn't Gretchen,* he told himself. He pulled her into a kiss, and at the moment their lips met, Will forced himself to think only of the present moment. Not the past, which he couldn't change, and barely understood. Not the future, which he couldn't guess at and which he had no control over. Just the floral scent of Gretchen's hair, the smoothness of her skin, the sweetness of her lips.

Just the now.

Chapter Eleven

From the Walfang Gazette
*Walfang Ghosts to Be Subject of
Documentary*

Citing a spate of local paranormal activity, Alex Kichida has announced plans to film the next installment of his *Phantasm* documentary series in the city. "*Phantasm* seeks to investigate several historical claims in and around the Walfang area," read an official press release. "Placed in the context of letters, diaries, and news clippings, the film hopes to substantiate the presence of several known ghosts."

Tom Stressland, Long Island historian, stated that there are several stories about apparitions that have become local legends. Moreover, the police department confirmed that there has been an increase in reported destruction of property that remains unexplained.

"Usually, unexplained nocturnal activity corresponds to an increase in the raccoon population," said Chief of Police Finbarr (Barry) McFarlan. "I'm not sure it's going to make for the most exciting documentary." But Kichida is undeterred. . . .

Gretchen sat in the kitchen, debating whether or not to heat up her lukewarm coffee, when a light rap at the front door made her nearly jump out of her chair. She'd had a restless night and had woken with the same ugly feeling of dread she'd felt so often lately, as if there was another presence in the room, someone watching her.

So she'd called Mafer.

"Hey, Gretchen," Mafer had said when she'd picked up the phone. "What's up?"

"Listen, can you come over?"

"Just tell me where you live," Mafer had replied, and that was the entire conversation.

Now Gretchen headed into the front hall, but her father had already pulled open the door. He was laughing at something Mafer had said.

"Gretchen!" Johnny said with a smile. "Your friend is here."

"Hi." Mafer gave Gretchen a wink. She wore a long, thin gray scarf looped around her neck, plus her usual off-white jacket. "I'm here and ready for action."

"Are you two working on a project?" Johnny asked.

Mafer turned to Gretchen with lifted eyebrows.

"Yes," Gretchen said.

"Okay, well, have fun." Johnny beamed from one girl to the other like a goofy dad on a 1950s sitcom. It made Gretchen want to laugh, but also touched her heart. Her father worried about her, she knew that. He wished she had more female friends. He was more delighted by Mafer's presence than Gretchen was.

"Come on upstairs," Gretchen said.

Mafer followed her down the cramped hallway and

up the stairs. "Hm," she said when she stepped into Gretchen's room.

"What is it?" Gretchen asked. She closed the door behind them, cognizant that her father might be below them, listening.

"You're messy," Mafer noted, which made Gretchen laugh. "I just wasn't expecting that. You seem like the tidy type."

Gretchen looked at her desk, strewn with charcoal and an open sketchpad. There were clothes and books all over the floor. The bottom of her closet was littered with shoes, one on top of the other like rats jumbled in a cage. At least her bed was made—crooked, though, and lumpy. "I can be tidy sometimes," Gretchen said.

Mafer took off her scarf and jacket and dropped them both onto Gretchen's bed. She crossed to the window and looked out. "You can see the house next door."

"Will lives there."

Mafer didn't react to this news. *Perhaps she knew it already,* Gretchen mused as her friend walked over to the bookcase. "Oh," Mafer said suddenly. She rubbed her arms, shivering, and looked over at Gretchen. She peered at the ceiling. "Not good."

"What?"

"I don't know. Something."

"Something?"

Mafer locked eyes with her. "There's a presence here."

Gretchen nodded. "That's why I called."

Mafer rubbed her arms again and frowned at the corner of the ceiling. Then she walked over to Gretchen's bed and perched on the end of it. "Are you afraid?"

"Sometimes," Gretchen admitted. She was still standing near her bureau, unsure whether to sit down. "Should I be?"

"Maybe." Mafer cocked her head. "So, what do you want?"

Gretchen sighed, and she felt as if all of the air whooshed out of her at once. "I don't know. I want it to go away, I guess."

"We could ask it to leave."

"Will that work?"

Mafer shrugged. "I don't know. What else should we do?" Her dark eyes watched Gretchen, serious, unafraid. Gretchen realized that she had been hoping that Mafer would have an answer—that she would be psychic enough to know what to do.

"There isn't some way to get rid of it?" Gretchen's voice was almost pleading.

Mafer giggled, then clamped her hands over her mouth. "I'm sorry. I don't mean to laugh. It's just—I'm not a witch, or something. I just get feelings. I know things. That's all. I don't have, like, mysterious powers. If there's something here, I can't just order it around. I don't even know if I can talk to it."

"Could you try?"

She glanced up at the ceiling. "Yeah, okay. Do you have a candle?"

Gretchen went down the hall to the bathroom and

brought back the scented candle she'd bought the year before and a box of matches.

"Ooh, gingerbread." Mafer sniffed the candle, and Gretchen couldn't help wishing that her friend would be more serious, or mysterious, or magical, or something. She wished that they had a beeswax candle, or maybe a scent like sage.

But Mafer didn't protest that she couldn't talk to a spirit with a gingerbread candle. She just sat down on the floor and lit the wick without any fanfare.

Gretchen settled across from Mafer as the wick caught. Mafer blew out the match, and the smell of sulfur filled the air. Mafer watched the smoke rise from the charred splinter and then looked at Gretchen. "Did you see that?" she asked.

"The smoke?"

"The face," Mafer replied.

"No," Gretchen admitted.

Mafer shrugged. Then she shut her eyes. It was late morning, and light streamed in through the window. It didn't seem like the proper setting for a séance. *Is that what we're having?* Gretchen wondered. *A séance?* The word raised images of slumber parties and eight-year-olds. *I'm such an idiot. What am I doing?*

"We sense your presence," Mafer said aloud. "Is there something you would like to tell us?"

Gretchen waited, but she didn't know what for: for the windows to blow out, for books to fly off the shelves, for the walls to bleed? But none of that happened. Nothing happened at all. Mafer just sat still.

Then, suddenly, the candle flared. Gretchen's heart leaped into her throat, and she had to strangle a scream.

"Please leave this place." Mafer's voice was firm.

It was then that Gretchen realized that her friend wasn't simply sitting there, motionless. She was listening. Mafer could hear something. Or she thought she could.

Gretchen's whole body was tensed, like an animal that fears it may have to dart away at any moment. After what seemed like an age, Mafer opened her eyes. She blew out the candle and ran her hands through her long dark hair.

"Did you—did you hear anything?" Gretchen asked.

"Yes."

"Is it gone?"

"No."

"No?" Gretchen wasn't prepared for this answer. Tears burned behind her eyes; her throat swelled.

"Gretchen." Mafer reached out and took her hand and pressed it reassuringly. "It wants to protect you."

"Protect me?" Gretchen's voice was almost a shriek. "That thing is scaring the crap out of me!" She thought about the golden-eyed waterspout, the attacking dog. "It tried to kill me!"

Mafer shook her head. "Not this presence."

"How do you know?"

She looked down at the floor. "I just know."

"Who is it?"

Mafer pressed her lips together, then looked Gretchen full in the face. "The spirit doesn't communicate in that way. Like I said, I get feelings. I know things. That's all. It's someone who cares for you and wants to protect you—that's all I'm sure about."

Gretchen studied her friend's face. Mafer looked pale and tired, as if communicating with the dead had sapped her. Mafer held her gaze a moment longer, then looked away. There was something about the way that Mafer had held her eyes that felt forced, and once the gaze was broken, Gretchen was besieged by doubt. How did she know whether Mafer was telling the whole truth?

Mafer stood up and walked over to the window. "Whose room is that?" she asked, gesturing toward the house across the creek. "Across from yours?"

"Will's. Tim's was on the third floor."

Mafer nodded. "You and Will are close. You've been close a long time."

Gretchen felt herself blush, and Mafer cocked her head but didn't ask why. Perhaps it was obvious.

"You trust him," Mafer said, but Gretchen sensed that the statement was more of a question.

"Of course."

Mafer nodded and returned her steady, thoughtful gaze to the window, and again Gretchen had to wonder at the inner workings of her friend's mind. It seemed unfair that Mafer knew things that other people didn't. How did she decide what to share and what to hide?

*   *   *

"How's it going?" Gretchen asked as she stepped behind the counter.

"Fine." Kirk shut his notebook with a snap, closing the door on another distressing image of a shadow-eyed woman. His huge dark eyes looked guilty, but Gretchen couldn't imagine why. So far he'd been an ideal busboy, efficient and unobtrusive. Even Angel had said that Kirk was "doing better than expected." Nobody minded if he snatched a moment or two to work on his drawings. But Gretchen couldn't think of a way to bring this up without embarrassing him. She shifted her weight awkwardly. "That's good. Listen, we're closing up soon. You can take off after you go bus table twelve."

"All right." Kirk grabbed the gray tub and headed for one of the booths that lined the side of the diner.

Gretchen got to work filling sugar jars. She jumped as someone banged on the door. "We're closed!" she shouted reflexively, reaching for a rag to wipe up the sugar that had spilled on the counter.

"But I'm giving you the big, sad eyes!" Angus pressed his face up against the glass. "I'm looking so adorable that you can't possibly resist me!"

"Don't let anybody in!" Angel called from behind his window as Gretchen moved toward the door.

"This isn't anybody, believe me," Gretchen said as she twisted the lock and pulled the door open.

"Thanks! Hi, Angel!" Angus waved cheerfully.

Angel frowned beneath his red mustache. "I'm not hanging around here all night."

"I'm doing great, thanks!" Angus chirped. He turned back to Gretchen. "I was just down at the *Gazette*. Had a meeting with *Dahlila Jackson*." He waggled his eyebrows, as if Gretchen should be impressed.

"Who's that?" Gretchen asked.

"What? It's Dahlila Jackson! *The* Dahlila Jackson. Hello, Pulitzer Prize winner? *New York Times?* Ring any bells?" Angus hopped onto a stool and reached over the counter, helping himself to a coffee mug.

"No," Gretchen said.

"Well, she's a big deal," Angus explained, waving his empty mug. "She had a nervous breakdown and moved out to Walfang. Now she's recovered and is taking over the editor-in-chief spot at the *Gazette*."

"And she wanted to meet with you at ten at night?"

"Newspapers have crazy deadlines. Even small-time newspapers."

Gretchen took the mug and filled it with coffee, then handed it back to Angus.

He took a sip. "Wow! Love the coffee here. It's like getting slapped in the face."

"I'd be happy to give you a real slap in the face," Angel offered.

"Don't be so cranky," Angus told him.

"How can I not be cranky when I'm missing my favorite TV show?" Angel demanded.

"So go home," Angus told him. "What are you waiting around for?"

"Gretchen has to count the drawer," Angel grumbled, "then I've got to take the money to the bank."

"I'm almost finished." Gretchen popped open the

cash register and started counting one-dollar bills. She had already counted and recorded the larger bills. Next up was the change.

"Why can't Gretchen take the money to the bank?" Angus asked.

"She might get mugged," Angel growled. "It's not safe."

"I'll walk with her," Angus volunteered.

"You?" Angel scoffed.

"Sure. Why not?" Angus drained the last of his coffee. "I'm full of energy after this mug of tar."

Gretchen smiled at Angel's dubious expression. He clearly couldn't think of any reason that Angus shouldn't escort her to the bank. After all, he was over six feet tall and well built, and his uncle was the chief of police in Walfang. Besides, the town wasn't exactly a hub of crime activity.

"Fine," Angel said at last. Then, as an afterthought, he added, "Thanks."

"You see?" Angus whispered as Angel left through the rear door. "Nobody can resist my charms."

"Hm," Gretchen replied. She went on counting the dimes.

"So—where was I? Oh, right. Editor of the *Gaz.* Anyway, Dahlila told me that I should feel free to submit stories to the paper for possible publication." Angus cleared his throat importantly. "That is a direct quote, my friend. Straight from the top."

"Twenty-three pennies," Gretchen mumbled, recording the number on the deposit slip. "Are you an intern again?"

"Nah, but this might even be better. I can get some clips, put them in with my college applications . . ." Angus droned on.

Gretchen glanced at the final tally on the receipt. Off by thirty cents. That irritated her, but she wasn't about to recount the drawer. *Close enough,* she told herself. She looked around, but the diner was empty. *Kirk must have slipped out while I was counting the drawer.*

Gretchen took Angus's empty mug and washed it out. Then she went and locked the back door while Angus flipped off the lights. The only illumination came from the red neon Bella's Diner sign outside, and it cast strange shadows over the booths as she tucked the blue vinyl deposit bag under her arm. Gretchen could hear the neon buzz as she opened the door, let Angus step through, and locked it behind them.

"Everything looks different in the dark," Angus observed.

An image of Kirk's drawing—the eyes in shadow, endlessly watching—popped into Gretchen's mind. "I know what you mean," she said.

Their footsteps echoed, breaking the silence as they walked up the street. Walfang was a tourist town, and after Labor Day the September nights were quiet, even Saturday nights. In August, the streets would have been alive with activity.

The bank drop vault was a block and a half away. It was a small steel door set in the side of the wall— Gretchen had never noticed it before she began closing at Bella's. All you did was open the box with the key, pull down the handle, and drop the vinyl bag into the slot. Easy as sending a letter or returning books to the library. Then you locked the door again, and the deposit would sit safely at the bank until morning.

Up the street, the lights at the *Gazette* offices glowed brilliantly. Gretchen had never thought about the kind of hours that journalists keep before. But there they were, grinding away, checking facts, following up on leads, and they would keep on doing that, even after everyone else in town was fast asleep and dreaming. . . .

"Angus," Gretchen asked suddenly, "would you look into something for me?"

Angus fiddled with the zipper on his olive-green jacket. "Sure. What?"

"Would you find out some information about someone? She would have been living in Boston about seventeen years ago. Her name is Saskia Robicheck."

"How do you spell that?"

Gretchen told him, and he nodded but didn't bother to make a note. He hadn't asked why she needed the information—maybe he didn't care. Or maybe he didn't need to. She wasn't sure why she said it, but she whispered, "Don't tell Will," and Angus nodded as though he understood completely.

They walked on in silence for a while. "So how much is in there?" Angus asked, nodding at the bank bag beneath Gretchen's arm.

"Wouldn't you like to know."

"Enough to run off to Belize?"

Gretchen laughed. "Enough to run off, maybe, but not to come back."

Angus's grin was visible in the light of a street lamp. "Why would we want to come back?"

"Maybe because we don't speak the language and wouldn't be able to get jobs?" Gretchen suggested.

"They speak English in Belize," Angus said. "It used to be ruled by the British. Like Grenada."

"Why do you know that?"

Angus shrugged. "Because I'm incredibly sophisticated and cosmopolitan."

Gretchen was about to reply, but there was a sudden explosion of footsteps, then Angus let out a shout and lunged to protect her. He stumbled—knocking against Gretchen—as someone landed a fierce blow on his shoulder. Angus hit back, and the man staggered backward for a moment—far enough for Gretchen to see his face, which was twisted in a complex arrangement of hatred, fear, and madness. The man raised his arm, and Gretchen saw a weapon gleam in the low light from the bank's sign. The man turned to her.

"Hey!" Angus shouted.

In an instant, Gretchen felt flame whip through her, igniting her like dry tinder. Her body went numb and she couldn't feel her limbs, but she could see them moving. She watched like a bystander as she stepped forward and grabbed the man's arm. Her hand glowed with the subtle orange of a rising sun, as if it were lit from within, and the man screamed in agony. She heard the snap of bone, and the gun clattered to the pavement. And then she saw herself hit the man in the chest, sending him reeling, sprawling onto the cement ten feet from them.

Pain pierced her skull, forcing Gretchen to her knees.

"Are you okay?" Angus asked, kneeling before her.

No, she thought. She felt weak, nauseated . . . and confused. She touched her temple. No wound. It was just a headache so fierce that it felt like an injury. "Get the gun," she whispered. She looked down at her arm, which was still illuminated, as if blown with stardust. A moment later, it faded and became merely the pale shadow of light skin in darkness.

Angus clearly hadn't noticed—his attention was focused elsewhere. He grabbed the gun. "Shit!" he shouted. "Hot!" He managed to wrap his hand in his shirt and hold the gun that way as the man struggled to his feet. "Don't move," Angus shouted.

The man's smile was eerie, haunting. "You don't even know how to use it," he hissed.

Angus flipped off the safety. "My entire family is a bunch of cops, asshole."

The man hesitated. He started toward them, and a dark figure leaped from a tree.

"Shit!" Angus shouted as the figure landed on the man, knocking him to the ground. Angus took aim at the shadowy figure, who backed away, immediately raising his hands in surrender. Large, dark eyes stared at them in fear.

"Kirk!" Gretchen cried.

"Oh my God." Angus's arm fell to his side. "I nearly killed you, dude."

Kirk looked at them for a moment, then turned and ran off.

"Kirk!" Gretchen called after him. "Kirk!"

"Let him go," Angus said, sounding weary. "God, why is he always in a tree?" He pulled a cell phone from his pocket.

"Are you calling 911?"

"No, I thought I'd order a pizza," Angus said as he punched three numbers into the cell. "All of this crime fighting really works up an appetite."

Her weak laugh made the pain return to Gretchen's temple. She sucked in a breath. Angus gave their location, and Gretchen knew it would take only moments for the Walfang police to arrive in a cruiser.

The man let out a low moan. His hand hung at a strange angle, and Gretchen wondered if she had broken it.

The light from the street lamp shone on his face. In his state of semiconsciousness, he didn't look as threatening. He was white, in his forties, with a receding hairline and a pockmarked face.

Angus hung up and studied the man. "I feel like I know that guy."

"How could you know him?" Gretchen asked.

"Small town," Angus said. "Maybe I've seen him in the police station."

Gretchen nodded. It was possible. Anything was possible.

Pity clutched at her chest, and she hoped that she hadn't hurt him too badly. In the dark, he had seemed so menacing. Now he looked like a normal person, the kind of man you see at the grocery store, or someone who holds the door for you at the dentist's office.

Everything looks different in the dark, Angus had said.

Yes, Gretchen thought. *Everything.*

Chapter Twelve

From the Walfang Gazette
Police Blotter

Authorities were called to the house of Mary Walters last night at 9:47 p.m., where a suspect was engaged in vandalizing property. Shaun Walters, son of Mary Walters, had locked himself in his room, and was heard destroying the furniture therein. Ms. Walters had her son taken in for emergency psychiatric evaluation. . . .

The minute the Gremlin pulled into the driveway, Will darted out of his room. It was almost two in the morning, and he had been waiting for Gretchen to get home. Waiting, and trying not to worry. Unsuccessfully.

She hadn't replied to any of his calls, any of his texts.

But what could he do about it?

He had spent his time staring out his window at the house across the creek. The wooden shingle siding was a pale smudge against the darkness. The charcoal outline of the trees stood sentry against the starry sky. As usual, a soft yellow light spilled from a window in the corner, casting illumination on the gate and grass beyond. Every now and again, the breeze would carry a few notes as far as Will's open window. Will remembered how, when his hearing was better, he would fall asleep to the sounds of Johnny's music.

The scene would have been tranquil to most eyes, but to Will's fearful mind, the house seemed more like a lighthouse at the center of rocky shallows, calling Gretchen back to uncertain moorings.

He wasn't sure why he felt so uneasy tonight, but the fear had been growing in him over the past several days and had finally reached a fever pitch. As the, minutes crawled by, Will watched the stillness for any sign of her. Every passing car made his heart leap with hope that she'd finally come home, and then came the inevitable disappointment as the headlights shone straight across the black asphalt and kept going, out of sight.

She was late. Late. And she wasn't answering her cell phone. His heart pulsed with the fear of what it might mean, and his mind struggled to keep up with rational thoughts: *She ran into a friend. She went to a midnight movie. She left her phone at home. Customers came in late; she had to stay. Angel and Lisette invited her over.* And on and on. A thousand possibilities, all perfectly reasonable, but none as compelling as the undefined fear that haunted him.

And that was why, when the Gremlin finally pulled into the driveway, Will darted out of his room before the headlights cut off. He rushed out the front door and across the side lawn, over the small bridge, and into Gretchen's yard.

She was still sitting in the driver's seat, her forehead pressed against the steering wheel. Will knocked against the window, and she turned her face to look at him.

"What happened?" he asked, yanking open the car door. His heart plummeted at the sight of her. Even in the darkness, he could see her despairing expression. The sleeve of her shirt was torn, her hair snarled. "What happened?" he repeated, trying to keep the desperate fear out of his voice.

Gretchen looked up at him from beneath her eyelashes, the intense blue of her eyes half hidden in shadow. "We were mugged."

"What?" Will knelt before her.

"Angus went with me to take the money to the bank," Gretchen explained. "And some guy ran up behind us—"

Will reached for her, pulling her into a hug, pressing her against him. Of all the possibilities, a mugging hadn't entered his consciousness. He kissed the top of her head, her wild dandelion hair, and stroked her back. "You must have been so scared."

"No," Gretchen replied. "I wasn't."

He pulled away from her then. "You weren't?"

"Not until afterward." She put a weary hand to her forehead. "Does that sound strange?"

Yes, he thought. "Not really."

Slowly she climbed out of the car. Will stood aside as the door creaked and slammed closed. "I'm so tired," Gretchen said, clinging to Will's arm. "I can't deal with telling my dad about this."

"I'll come inside with you."

"Would you?"

He squeezed her hand. "I'm not leaving."

"You're not?"

"I'll sleep on your floor." Gretchen laughed, but Will didn't smile. "I'm not joking."

He expected her to protest. But she just reached up and ran a light finger across the scar that slashed down his face. "You can stay," she said. "But you won't have to sleep on the floor."

Gretchen turned restlessly in her sleep, and Will brushed a lock of damp hair away from her forehead. He wondered what dreams stripped their way through her mind. It was strange to think what a mystery she was, this familiar girl, who for as long as he could remember had been as much a fixture of his summers as hunting for crabs or riding the Ferris wheel at the county fair. He knew her. He knew her thoughts, he could finish her sentences, and yet she was a world of mystery to him.

What a deep, impenetrable loneliness that was—to know someone, and to love her, and to realize that there were places locked inside her that you would never see. Lonelier still was the feeling that he could help her, if only he could reach inside her and know her secrets.

And perhaps she could help him, if she knew his.

But fear kept him from speaking. And that, too, was lonely.

Why didn't he speak? Will wasn't sure of the answer. Once or twice he had thought that perhaps he should tell her about what happened that night on the bay. But he didn't want to terrify her. Or maybe he didn't want to terrify himself. And the longer he waited, the harder it became to break his silence. If she ever asked him why he hadn't said anything when she woke up in the hospital, he would answer that he didn't feel he could speak about it—not then. It was too much.

And now?

Now it was still too much, but in a different way, because Will had finally realized that he loved Gretchen, loved her so much that it caused him physical pain to think of her harmed or afraid. So he sent up the walls and kept his secret locked away. And here he was, in her bed with her bare shoulder beneath his hand, and yet she was further from him than ever.

A moan escaped her parted deep red lips. Will worried that she might have a fever, as her skin felt warm beneath his fingertips. But it was warm in the room, with their bodies pressed together. He stole out of bed, careful not to let his movements wake her, and crossed over to the window. Pushing aside the curtains, he lifted the window and let in the cool night air. A breeze blew in, stirring the fabric and cooling his skin.

She turned over in the bed, and the blankets fell away from her. Will covered her with the sheet, then sat at the foot of the bed. He watched her for a long time. Then, restless, he pulled on some clothes and padded downstairs into the kitchen.

He didn't turn on the light, and when he opened the refrigerator door he was nearly blinded. He waited a moment for the shadows to become shapes, then reached for a pitcher of ice water. He poured some into a glass and drank, shivering, a rapid reversal from the heat he had just escaped. The house fell into darkness again as Will closed the refrigerator and walked down the hall and out onto the front porch.

It was early—five-fifteen by the clock on the kitchen microwave—and only the palest shade of gray had begun to light the horizon. Will liked this quiet time of day, when the earth seemed to be resting. The kitchen light was on at his house, of course—his mother was baking. She hadn't noticed yet that he wasn't in his bed. He wondered what she would say when she did.

"Gretchie?" The porch light snapped on overhead.

Johnny let out a surprised "Oh!" and Will stood to face him, blushing madly.

"Uh—"

"Oh," Johnny said, relaxing slightly, as if he had feared an intruder. "It's you." He shook his head, bleary-eyed and confused. "Why are you still here?" The question was half addressed to himself, and he rubbed his goatee as his eyes traveled down Will's rumpled, blushing form and to his bare feet, then back up to the glass in Will's hand. An idea seemed to break over Johnny's face, shifting his features. "Oh," he said slowly, now clearly unsure what his response should be.

Will was frozen in place and might have stood there forever, dying particle by particle, but a scream, followed by the sound of breaking glass, pierced the quiet darkness. It came from overhead—Gretchen's room.

Will reacted faster than Johnny, plunging past him and back into the house. He flew up the stairs and threw open the door to Gretchen's room. Light and heat blasted from the doorway—her room was on fire.

"Call 911!" Will shouted to Johnny. Falling to his knees to avoid the smoke, he crawled into Gretchen's room.

Everything was in flames—the books on her desk, the curtains, the rug—and she stood in the center of her burning bed, in her thin nightgown, staring blankly. As she looked at him, she seemed to snap out of a trance. "Will?" She looked around her, clearly disoriented and frightened.

"Gretchen!" he shouted, and he stood, reaching for her wrist. But it was hot, and he cried out in pain. "Get down!"

She leaped over the flames and crawled behind Will to the door. They ran down the stairs, and Will grabbed a blanket from the couch and wrapped it around her as they headed outside.

"Oh, God, where's Daddy?" Gretchen asked. Will started back inside the house, but a moment later, Johnny appeared carrying Bananas. He set the cat down and pulled Gretchen into a hug. "The fire department is on its way."

Gretchen looked up at her window. Flames were still visible, the curtains nearly disintegrated in the heat. "I did that," she whispered.

"It wasn't your fault." Johnny stooped a little to look her in the eye. "It wasn't."

But Gretchen wrenched her eyes from his. Will felt her seeking his glance, and he forced himself to look at her, even though every fiber of his body revolted at what he knew she would say next.

"I did that," Gretchen repeated. "But I don't know how."

Chapter Thirteen

*"Tim!" Gretchen cried, but he was
calling to someone else—the other figure
on the boat.*

*Will. He looked up at Tim, and
at that moment, a movement caught
Gretchen's eye. Something surfaced. It
looked like a head, half out of the water
near the boat. The full moon shone
down, casting the eyes in shadow.*

Bananas sat on Gretchen's lap, purring contentedly,
as if nothing had happened. Gretchen was perched in
the corner of the Archers' stiff couch, an uncomfortable beast that had nothing—not even excellent
looks—going for it. The family's living room was oddly
formal, with a dark wood bowlegged coffee table and a
faux Tiffany lamp. It was strange, because the furniture was so at odds with the comfortable, easy nature
of the family itself. Gretchen guessed that the furniture was part of an inheritance. Maybe it had been in
the house longer than any of the current inhabitants.
But the furniture made the sitting room into something like a fancy shoe—it looked all right, but it wasn't
comfortable—and so it went mostly unused.

Gretchen knew how that could be. There were
things she owned that she didn't use and thus didn't
think about. She had been surprised how many had

appeared when she packed up her room in Manhattan. A jeweled belt, a pair of red patent stilettos, a long purple Indian skirt—all fragments of personae abandoned. Gretchen liked to think that she was getting better and better at finding things that reflected the person she was on the inside. The trouble was, that person kept changing.

Mr. Archer had arrived at the Ellis house only moments after the fire trucks had. Gretchen had been clutching Bananas, standing between Johnny and Will on the front lawn. They were watching as smoke poured from Gretchen's broken window. Firefighters ignored them, going in and out of the house in businesslike fashion. Their heavy clothing and helmets made Gretchen think of army ants, who can carry twenty times their own weight.

"Cat's not stuck in a tree, I see," Mr. Archer drawled in his dry way.

Johnny turned and looked at his old friend, whose broad hand was on his shoulder. "Problem in Gretchen's room."

Mr. Archer looked troubled but not surprised.

Will said quickly, "These things are usually electrical."

"You sure got here fast," his father said to him, and Will clamped his mouth shut.

Gretchen couldn't tear her eyes from the smoke. *That fire,* she thought, *is not electrical. It's me. I caused it.*

She was sure of it.

I get upset, and things burst into flames.

It was a simple explanation, and although it seemed impossible, there was no other explanation that worked. *It may not make sense,* Gretchen thought. *It may not seem possible. But that's what it is.*

The edge of the sky was orange, fading to lilac over-head as the sun prepared for yet another dramatic entrance. Gretchen wondered what time it was. "Why don't you all come on over for a while?" Mr. Archer suggested. "These guys will finish up here." He didn't wait for a response, just walked over to the nearest firefighter. Gretchen watched as Mr. Archer indicated his house and the firefighter nodded.

Mr. Archer walked back to them. "Let's see what Evelyn has cooked up."

Johnny and Mr. Archer walked side by side in companionable silence, and Gretchen, still clinging to her cat, trailed behind them with Will. Bananas strug-gled, and Gretchen hoisted her half over her shoulder so that the orange cat was looking backward, toward the Ellis house. Bananas hissed once, then settled down.

"He said there isn't much damage. Mostly smoke in Gretchen's room; that's all."

Johnny just shook his head. He looked over his shoulder at Gretchen, saw her watching him, then turned back to Mr. Archer. "Could have been worse."

"A lot worse," Mr. Archer agreed.

They walked in through the front door, and Gretchen set Bananas onto the Persian carpet in the hallway.

The cat promptly strutted off, as if she owned the place.

The house was filled with the sweet scent of cinnamon and browning sugar. From May to October, Evelyn woke up early to make scones and quick breads for the farm stand, then went back to bed around eight for a few hours.

"Sit here," Mr. Archer said, indicating the stiff sitting room furniture. "I'll go talk to Evelyn. Will, come help out."

Johnny and Gretchen looked at each other uncertainly as Mr. Archer and Will stepped through the kitchen door. Gretchen heard Mrs. Archer's voice ask, "What is going on over there?" Mr. Archer muttered something that Gretchen couldn't catch.

Johnny sighed and perched at the edge of the overstuffed wing chair. His long legs made him look like an awkward spider. Gretchen sat down on the couch, and Evelyn bustled in with a plate of muffins. "The whole world's gone crazy," she said as she held the platter out to Gretchen.

"Thank you." Gretchen took a carrot raisin muffin, and Mrs. Archer touched a strand of Gretchen's hair.

"I'm so glad you're all right," Mrs. Archer said.

"Thank you," Gretchen said again, more awkwardly this time. Gretchen felt guilty for adding to Mrs. Archer's worry.

A firefighter knocked at the door, and Will pulled it open.

"We're about done," the firefighter announced.

"There's an insurance adjuster at your house," he added to Johnny.

"Got here pretty fast," Mr. Archer noted, and Johnny nodded.

"I'll go talk to him."

Gretchen started up, but her father waved her back to her seat. "I'll take care of it. You stay here."

Once Johnny left, Mr. and Mrs. Archer hovered around for a while. Mrs. Archer kept trying to stuff Gretchen with muffins; Mr. Archer just sat still as a bone in his chair. Finally he had to get started on his work, and Evelyn had to head back to bed. Gretchen was left alone with Will.

A long silence coursed through the room as Will sat pressed into the far corner of the couch. Bananas reappeared and leaped onto Gretchen's lap. Gretchen stroked her ears, and the cat settled down happily.

"Tell me about that fire on the bay," Gretchen said.

Will studied his hands. "There was a fuel spill. The gas ignited."

"How did it ignite?"

Will looked at her sharply. "Don't."

"Quit lying to me."

"I'm not lying."

"Not telling me is the same as lying!" Gretchen turned, and Bananas rolled over ridiculously, asking for a belly rub, oblivious to the tension in the room. "I already know the answer, so just say it."

Will looked at her for a long time, the expression in his denim-blue eyes flat. He picked at a loose thread in the fabric on the arm of the couch. Finally he seemed to reach a decision. "I don't know what happened that night."

Gretchen stood up, dumping Bananas onto the floor. "You need to stop protecting me, Will, and start helping me."

She walked right out the front door and didn't look back.

Chapter Fourteen

From Fury Poems, *by Chandrama Soleil*

She carries the brand, she carries the flame,
To take you to Hell, and back again.

Gretchen fought a sense of vertigo as she walked down the school hallway. The movement and chatter around her set her on edge, and she felt like a lost salmon, swimming the wrong way, as she slogged to her locker.

Sunday had passed in a fog. Her room was ruined. Everything smelled of smoke or was damp and covered in fire extinguisher foam. The fire had started near her bed (of course it had) and lit up her linens in a sudden conflagration, but it hadn't spread that much. Still, not much was salvageable, and Gretchen found herself grieving for her lost things—her sketchpad, her quilt, even her fuzzy slippers and ancient pillow. Her father had taken her to the outlet mall half an hour away, and when she had protested, he'd waved away her concerns about money. "A girl needs clothes," he'd said. "Besides, we have insurance."

Johnny was one of those men who knew that women needed things but had no idea what those things were, so he retreated to the food court and played with his smartphone while Gretchen wandered around the stores, trying to find a few items that weren't hopeless. The outlets were often the last resort, the place where more adventurous styles went to die. But she finally found a store that had some jeans and simple sweaters. Normally she might have looked for something more stylish, but she just couldn't make herself care.

She bought socks. She bought underwear. She bought shoes, feeling angry that she had to spend money on these things. *The government should just issue this stuff to people,* she thought. *Make them standard. Why should I have to waste energy picking it out?*

And when she got home, exhausted, she couldn't go to her room. She couldn't even go to her *home.* They were going to stay with the Archers for a few days. Evelyn had offered Gretchen Tim's room—it was in the attic, and easily had the nicest view in the neighborhood—but Gretchen's look of horror must have been obvious, because Mrs. Archer backed off completely and Johnny took that room. Gretchen got the guest room. That was fine with her. It was very basic: a full-sized bed and a bureau, a mirror, a chair to sit in. Bananas leaped up and curled between the navy blue pillows arranged against the headboard as Gretchen shoved her new clothes into drawers, not bothering to cut off the tags.

Then she'd tried to take a nap. But her mind whirled with the memory of the night of the fire. She'd had a vivid dream that had hung on the edges of her mind, just waiting for her to rest before launching a full-fledged attack. But when she rested, the dream returned to her, not as a dream but as a memory, one she couldn't stop:

She was standing on the shore, looking out at the dark water, a sky full of stars overhead. The full moon shone down on the water, sending a river of light across the still ocean. And there, gliding across the illuminated surface, was a sailboat. The two sails were full, two figures visible on deck.

Gretchen looked down at her feet. They were bare, and she dug her toes into the soft, pale sand. She did not wonder what she was doing there. She knew—she had sleepwalked out of the house, across the Archer property, and down to the water.

She looked back at the sailboat and saw a figure standing rigid as a soldier on deck. It was as if something had caught his attention out over the water. He called out, and Gretchen realized that the figure was Tim.

She didn't find this strange. Instead, a wave of guilt washed over her. The last time they had spoken, she had told him that she did not love him. He had been kind—more than kind—but she knew that his heart was broken.

"Tim!" she cried, but he was calling to someone else—the other figure on the boat.

Will. He looked up, and at that moment, a movement caught Gretchen's eye. Something surfaced. It looked like a head, half out of the water near the boat. The full moon shone down, casting the eyes in shadow.

With a shout, Tim reached down. The figure lifted her arm, dripping, from the water. Her skin was pale,

and her long fingers ended in dagger-like nails. Something about the movement made Gretchen's breath
catch in her throat. She wanted to cry out, but found
she couldn't make a sound.

The figure pulled Tim into the water with a splash.

Will shouted and rushed to help his brother, but
another figure burst through the water. She landed on
deck, blocking Will's path. She wore animal skins and
smiled slowly, revealing teeth sharpened to shark
points. Her dark hair streamed behind her in wild
ropes as she stepped toward Will. He stumbled backward and made as if he might jump into the water.
But now the river of light was dotted with rising
heads. . . .

Tim surfaced for a moment, screaming, and Will
lunged at the Siren. But she slashed him across the
face, opening a deep gash that blinded him with blood.

Tim's screams disappeared as the things dragged
him back down, and the Siren leaped forward, clutching Will in her long arms. She wrapped an arm around
his neck in an attempt to crush the life from him.

And then Gretchen heard herself keening. She felt
as if her blood had caught fire in her veins, and she
was running, running—running right out over the
water. So fast she did not sink.

A hideous shriek fell from Gretchen's lips—a
primeval sound—and she saw the look of surprise,
then fear, on the Siren's face as Gretchen lunged on
board.

The Siren released Will and stumbled backward.

She whispered something in a hoarse, guttural voice as Will lay gasping and coughing on the slick wood.

The word reached down into the depths of her memory. Somehow Gretchen knew it was a name, and she answered, "Yes."

Then the Siren looked her up and down, taking in the nightgown, the youth of Gretchen's face. She spoke strange words and laughed a slow, vicious chuckle, and Gretchen felt something harden in her then, as if she had been cast around a core of steel. There were two minds at work within her. One she recognized as her own, which swirled with fear and confusion. But there was another, unknown mind. This mind was not afraid.

The Siren sprang at her, knocking Gretchen against the mast. Gretchen cried out in pain as fire ripped through her body. Behind her, the sail burst into flame. Gretchen clasped the seekrieger as the surface of the water reverberated with shrieks, then grew quiet as the Sirens fled at the sight of the flames.

But Gretchen did not loosen her grip on the Siren in her arms. She fought, struggling against Gretchen's grip, but Gretchen would not let go—not even when the Siren's scream threatened to deafen her. Finally the Siren reached for the mast. She held on to the wood, placing all of their weight against it, and the light craft began to tip.

Tim surfaced again. He was limp, though, in the arms of a pale-haired Siren. Still, at the sight of his brother, Will clawed his way across the deck.

"No!" Gretchen screamed as Will hauled himself over the edge of the sailboat.

The Siren redoubled her efforts, and the *Vagabond* rolled over on its side, dousing the flames.

Gretchen felt like a hot brand dipped into water to be cooled. She couldn't see Will, and some of her strength dissipated on the air, like steam.

Where is he? She searched the water as the Siren kicked against her, then knocked her head with a fierce elbow.

There. Gretchen released her grip and swam toward Will, who was kicking at the Siren who held his brother. Tim was dead, Gretchen could see that. Blood flowed from his open neck. A voice that was not her own cried, "Leave him!" as the Siren released Tim and landed a fierce blow against Will's ear, knocking him unconscious.

Gretchen reached for the Siren, but she was too quick, darting away in fear. Gretchen grabbed hold of Will and fought through the water to haul him to shore. Most of her superhuman strength had departed, but so had the Sirens. It was difficult, but she swam with him, dragging him to shore.

When they were safe on the sand, she pushed against his stomach and breathed into his mouth until he coughed and gasped for air. His hair was wet and filled with sand as she brushed it away from his face. A small trickle of blood dripped from his ear.

She looked out over the water, where the boat lay on its side. The sea was perfectly calm, as if nothing had ever happened. But Gretchen knew that Tim was there, somewhere below the surface.

Something slashed across her face then. She hit out as the smell of burning wood filled her nostrils. Someone shouted her name, and when the blackness cleared, she saw that she was in her room, after all. Will was there, and Gretchen looked around in confusion.

This was no dream.

Her room was on fire.

And then Will had appeared, knocking her out of her half-dream state and sweeping her out of her room.

But since that moment she had been convinced that the dream had been trying to speak to her and that Will was hiding something. He was a terrible liar, and on the Sunday morning that she confronted him, his face betrayed him.

She and Will had avoided each other for the rest of the day, but they had gone to great effort not to make it obvious. Their parents outnumbered them, after all, and no doubt would have tried to patch things up if they had realized that there was anything wrong. So Gretchen and Will joked with each other and kept things civil while others were in the room. And when they weren't, they retreated to opposite ends of the house.

So here she was, at school, dressed in new clothes from top to bottom, inside and out. Dark wash jeans, gray shirt, green corduroy jacket, black boots, black socks. Will had driven her there in silence, and once he had parked, she got out and walked toward the building without waiting for him. He didn't try to catch up to her.

Gretchen was a walking husk, something dried up, ready to blow away at the slightest breath. She felt like there was nothing tying her to earth. She was wearing unfamiliar clothes, walking among unfamiliar people, living in an unfamiliar room. Even her body felt foreign to her.

Who am I?

Who am I, really?

Fire's daughter, came the answer, like a slap. She stopped in her tracks.

Kirk rounded a corner, and she found herself face to face with this artist who drew shadowy, fearsome women half submerged in the bay. Gretchen didn't know how her dream was tied to the fire in her room, but she felt in her bones that everything—everything that was happening to her—was a piece of the same whole. "Tell me about your art," she said to Kirk.

His dark eyes widened and his straight black brows drew together. He clutched his fat history book closer to his chest as if it were a shield. "What?"

"Tell me about the face in the water," Gretchen pressed.

"I . . ." Kirk looked past her, as if for help, but nobody was paying attention to them. "I don't . . . Don't you know?"

"I'm not sure."

"The . . . the seekriegers. The ones you . . ." He winced. "The ones you killed."

Gretchen's mouth went dry suddenly, like a drop of water evaporating from the surface of a hot pan. *I misheard him,* she told herself. "What?"

Kirk cringed a little then, looking desperate. "The night you set the fire on the bay . . . you killed them. Asia, all of them. The Fury awoke."

"Asia?" What little there was tying her to the earth seemed to fall away, and Gretchen felt as if she would slide off the planet. "Asia?"

"Why are you doing this to me?" She realized that Kirk was trembling. A tear spilled from his right eye. "Why are you asking these things?" He was frightened, she could see that. "Maybe I'm . . . maybe I'm . . ." He put a hand to his head.

But she didn't have the energy to comfort him. She turned and started to run, but instead slammed into the person behind her, sending them both sprawling and books and notebooks tumbling to the floor. The students around them cleared away.

It was Will she had collided with.

Will looked at Kirk, then at Gretchen. "What's he saying?" Will demanded. "I saw you talking. What's he telling you?"

Kirk dashed away, and Gretchen felt herself grab Will's shirt collar. A hoarse whisper, barely more than a gasp: "Why didn't you tell me?" She scrambled down the hall, leaving her books where they were, and bolted through the double doors.

"Gretchen!"

She heard Will shouting her name, the echoes bouncing off tile walls, but the syllables died as the doors sighed closed behind her. She didn't even know where she was running to—all she knew was that she had to get away.

The air was cold, and it blew across her face as she ran down the steps. The doors thudded behind her, and she heard a shout—Will's voice. "Gretchen!"

She ran to the parking lot, but Will's legs were longer, and he ducked between her and the car door.

"Don't run away from me," he begged.

"What did he mean, Will?" She stared up at him, her whole body tense with the need to know the truth. "He said that I killed Asia." She stared into his eyes, which seemed to have darkened to a blue that was almost gray, like the edge of a thunderhead before it breaks into rain. She was trembling with two kinds of fear—the fear that Will might at last tell her the truth, and the fear that he might not. She felt the need for honesty like a drowning person needs air. "Did I kill her?"

"Gretchen . . ." Will ran his hand through his hair, exposing the scar that slashed across his face. He looked away from her, as if he was trying to form the right words.

"Don't think about it," Gretchen said. "Yes or no, Will."

His eyes fastened onto hers then. "No."

"No?" Her heart leaped, then felt itself straining, as if it had hit the confines of a cage. She didn't know whether or not to believe him.

"You . . . there was a fire . . ."

Gretchen heard these words and understood their meaning for the first time. "I set the fire."

Will looked at her, but he didn't answer.

"I set the fire," she repeated. "And I killed them."

"If you hadn't, we would both be dead. The only way to kill a Siren is with fire."

"Does that make it all right?"

He took her hand then, and lifted it to his lips. He kissed her palm gently, then pulled her to him. "You didn't mean to do it." His voice was a whisper. "You didn't even know you had done it. You fainted right afterward."

Gretchen felt her body relax against his. This, she knew, was the truth. Of course she had set the fire. That was the only answer. Her mind flashed on the memory she'd had—Will and Tim in the boat, under attack from seekriegers. The sail had burst into flame, and she had managed to save Will.

"I killed Asia." Tears flowed from her eyes, wetting the front of Will's blue plaid shirt. This was worse than when she thought Asia had simply died trying to save her. Far worse.

"There wasn't any other way, Gretchen," Will whispered into her hair. "You didn't even do it on purpose . . . but I would have."

"Why is this happening to me?"

She looked up at him, and he brushed the hair away from her face. "I don't know."

"I want it to stop."

"Maybe it will."

She looked away from him, a low flame of anger burning in her veins. She hated to admit it, but she was angry with him for finally telling the truth. No, she was angry that the truth was what it was. "Why didn't you tell me before?"

"What would I have said?"

"I don't know—the truth."

"Whatever that is."

"Don't joke, Will."

"I'm not."

He held up his hands, and his face looked so helpless that she was reminded of a time long ago when she and a seven-year-old Will had caught a fish. They had been trying all afternoon, and when a small blackfish finally nibbled the end of their line and they pulled it up, she had shrieked in horror, and Will had jumped back as the fish flapped wildly, desperate to be free.

"Put it back!" Gretchen had screamed, but Will didn't want to touch the fish, so she had finally grabbed it, unhooked the bleeding, gaping mouth from the silver hook, and tossed it back into the creek. "We almost killed it," she had said then, filled with remorse.

And that was how she felt now—as if her wish had finally been granted, but the granting was something horrible and terrifying. She knew the truth, but all she wanted was to toss it back. And nobody could help her.

"Let's go," Will said finally, taking her hand again.

"Where are we going?"

Will looked surprised. "Back to school."

"Are you serious?"

He smiled a little sadly. "What else are we supposed to do?" he asked.

This, too, was the truth, Gretchen realized. And so she slowly followed him back into the building, trying to make sense of her swimming thoughts and broken heart.

"Dudes, you are not going to believe this!" Angus said, sliding onto the orange chair beside Gretchen. He looked like he was about to say something, then got distracted by Will's lunch. "Gimme some of that." He broke off half of Will's chocolate chip cookie.

Will rolled his eyes.

"Man, what does your mom put in this—crack? How am I supposed to stop eating it?" He reached for the second half of the cookie.

"You could just say to yourself, 'Gee, this isn't my cookie, maybe I should stop eating it,'" Will suggested.

Angus laughed as he polished off the cookie and brushed the crumbs from his hands. He looked over at Gretchen, grinning, and she felt her body unspool a little. She was grateful for his presence. She and Will had just been sitting there in tense silence for the past five minutes. It had been wearing her out.

"So—did you want to tell us something?" Gretchen prompted.

"What?" Angus looked blank.

Will sat back in his chair. "You said that we wouldn't believe something."

"Oh, right!" Angus put up his hands, palms out, as if he were ready to stop traffic with his news. He turned to Gretchen. "The guy who robbed us killed himself."

Will let out a strangled "What?" and the pizza Gretchen had just consumed threatened to make its way back up her throat. For a moment she felt as if she had flown out of her body—like she was watching herself from above, hearing the news. She had no sensation in her hands, her feet. Her body was a strange, unreal thing.

And then Angus said, "Crazy, right?" like he was discussing some wild celebrity gossip, and Gretchen fell back to earth, crashing into her body like a meteor. She went concave, her body collapsing like a roof under a heavy weight of snow.

"Jesus, Angus, you can't just drop that on someone." Will was watching Gretchen, concern stamped across his face.

"Sorry—I'm sorry." Angus touched Gretchen's arm. "Hey, I'm sorry." He leaned down to look up into her face. "I didn't know you'd be so upset."

"Anyone with a heart would be upset, Angus." Will's voice was sharp.

Gretchen forced herself to take a deep breath. Then another. It was a while before she felt like she could speak. "What—what happened?"

Angus hesitated a moment. He looked over at Will,

who shook his head slightly. But the question had been asked. "He hanged himself," Angus said quietly. "In his cell. He used a bedsheet."

Gretchen digested this information. She didn't know why, but for some reason she looked over at Kirk, who was watching her intently. There was something in his expression that made her wonder if he knew what they were talking about.

"I don't feel well," Gretchen said.

"I'll get you a glass of water." Will stood and hurried to the drinks counter for a plastic cup.

"I'm sorry, Gretchen," Angus said. The spray of freckles across his nose had faded but were still visible, and his wide face and large eyes were so childlike that she couldn't help forgiving him. "Listen . . ." He shifted uncomfortably in his seat, then looked at her evenly. "I am now going to drop another bomb on you, so I just want you to be prepared."

She closed her eyes for a moment, trying to focus as her heart did a skip-thump. "Okay," she said slowly.

Angus cleared his throat. He took a deep breath, like someone who has accepted his fate, and reached into his pocket. "That thing you asked me about." The paper was folded into messy quarters, and he laid it on the table before her. "Weird story, actually."

They both looked at the paper for a moment without moving.

Gretchen touched a protruding corner with a finger, then gingerly unfolded it. Angus had photocopied the article. It was crooked on the page, and for some reason that bothered her.

One Lost, One Found After Fire
Brookline, MA

A conflagration at 657 Attinson
Street, just above the Juliet Theater, is
feared to have claimed a life last night.
Saskia Robicheck, age unknown, is missing and presumed dead. Investigators
have not yet found any remains, nor have
they determined the cause of the fire.

"Most fires of this nature are caused
by electrical problems," Fire Chief Law-
rence Sawyer commented this morning.
"I strongly urge everyone to get a thor-
ough inspection—especially anyone living in one of the older houses out here."

But adding mystery to tragedy is the
presence of a small baby at the scene of
the fire. The baby has been taken into
care at Mercy General Hospital, but
doctors there have stated that the child is
in good health and seems unharmed by
the fire. "She must have been placed
there after the fire," said Dr. Elizabeth
Anders. "She's only a few hours old."

The firefighter on the scene was
flummoxed as to how the baby might
have gotten there. "It was so strange—
the baby was in the part of the house that
had already burned most completely,"
said firefighter DeShawn Greene. "She
was surrounded by black, smoking
ashes."

Gretchen scanned the article, but there wasn't
much more information. She took a second glance at
the date at the top: July 21, 1995. "The day after my

birthday," she said. It wasn't that she was surprised, not exactly. This just confirmed what she had feared all along. "Saskia Robicheck is my mother," Gretchen told him. "My birth mother."

"I didn't even know you were adopted."

Gretchen shrugged. "Why would you?"

He sighed. "You think you're the baby?" Angus tapped the paper. "This baby?"

"I know I am," Gretchen said. She placed the paper carefully on the tabletop, folded it in half. She felt strange throwing it away, but she didn't really want to keep it. So she just folded it again and tucked it into her back pocket. "I just don't know what it means. If it means anything."

"It's just weird."

"Who knows what's weird anymore?" Gretchen pushed back in her chair and folded her arms across her chest. She was silent.

"So, does this mean you have magic powers, or something?" Angus joked. "Like some Stephen King *Firestarter* deal? Like, maybe you could open a barbecue place and—"

"Please stop."

"Okay."

Gretchen pressed her fingers against her temples, fighting to contain the thoughts that pinged around her mind. "I don't know what it means," she said at last. "Thanks for looking it up, though." She started to stand.

"Gretchen." Angus grabbed her hand, forcing her to stop. "I'm sorry."

And he did look so sorry that she felt awful for him. Gretchen gave his hand a squeeze. "It's not your fault." She was careful to make her voice gentle, despite the fear and anger that raged inside her.

"No, but . . . I'm still sorry. I can see you're freaked out. But this doesn't mean anything."

Angus stood and leaned forward to give her a hug. He was more than a head taller than she, and her head banged awkwardly into his shoulder, her nose mashing into the ridged line of the zipper on his jacket. Still, she was grateful for the contact.

"What's up?" Will asked. His head was cocked in bemusement at the sight of his friends hugging. He handed Gretchen a plastic cup filled with water. She felt him watching her as she took a sip. "Are you okay?" he asked.

"Yes."

She looked over at Angus, who touched her elbow. Will noticed the gesture and must have taken it as a sign that Angus was asking for forgiveness, because he sighed. "Okay," he said. "Good."

The bell rang, signaling the next class. "I'll see you guys," Gretchen said, scooping up her tray.

"See you," Will called after her. Angus was silent.

For once, she supposed, Angus didn't have anything else to say.

Chapter Fifteen

*Fireflies floated overhead, sailing
toward the black sky as if longing to join
the stars, then winked out. Around her,
faces—angry and dirty—glowered,
flickering in reflected torchlight. An old
woman in a gray head scarf shouted
something, but Gretchen couldn't hear
the words—it was as if she were
watching television with the sound
turned off. She could see that everyone
was crying out, screaming at once, but
Gretchen couldn't understand why.*

*Beside her was a man of about fifty,
with heavy-lidded eyes and sunken
cheeks. He stood tall, as straight as a
scarecrow, and lifted a bony finger at her.
He began to speak, but again Gretchen
couldn't hear the words. His lips formed
the word* burn *and she saw that he
carried a torch. It was then that she
realized that she was immobile—her
hands tied behind her back, her feet
resting on uneven ground. And then the
torch was thrust at her, and she saw the
kindling at her feet.*

*She tried to cry out but found herself
as soundless as the crowd gathered to
watch her burn. . . .*

"Uncle Carl?" Will called at the front door. He had been
hoping to catch his uncle alone for the past few days,

but whenever he did, Carl babbled on about some inane subject or found an excuse to leave as quickly as possible. Will had finally had to accept that he had to corner his uncle and force a few questions.

"Come on in!" a voice boomed at him from somewhere deep in the house.

Will pushed open the screen door—the main door was standing wide open—and stepped into the living room. Carl came in from the kitchen, wiping his left hand on a towel. His right hand was still wrapped in a bandage. He looked surprised, and maybe not too pleased, to see his nephew. "Will. What brings you by?"

"Just wanted to hang out."

Carl stood there, eyebrows lifted. "Oh. Okay, uh . . ." He gestured toward the kitchen, and Will followed him there. He sat down at the tiny table across from where Carl was sliding something into the oven.

"I didn't know you could cook," Will said.

"Miserable bachelors always know how to cook." Carl had been divorced for eight years. Will knew that he didn't often see his two daughters. Carl's ex-wife wasn't the kind to split amicably. She had more of a slash-and-burn personality.

Carl shut the oven door slowly, then folded the blue and yellow print towel and hung it over the handle. He looked down at the floor. "Um, Will. About the other night. I'm . . . I know my behavior hurt you, and—"

"Did you know that man?"

Carl seemed surprised by the question. "What man?"

"The one at the police station. The one who was singing."

"No." He mashed his lips together, as if he didn't trust himself to say more.

"No, but . . . ?" Will prompted.

Carl crossed the yellow linoleum, sat down in the chair across from Will. "I guess I knew that song he was singing."

"You seemed really upset by it."

"Will, I don't want to talk about this."

"I know, Uncle Carl. Believe me, I wouldn't be asking if it weren't important."

Carl's chair screeched as he pushed it back from the table, but he didn't stand up. Instead, he gazed at a far-off point—somewhere beyond what Will could see. "It's just—I used to hear these songs."

It was as if something had stolen the breath from Will's throat. He parted his lips, but nothing—no word, no breath—came through them.

"That's when I started drinking. I'd drink until I passed out, just to make the song go away. And then . . . I don't know . . . I did quit drinking, and everything turned around . . . and the song went away by itself. And then I thought I heard it again the other night." Carl looked down at his injured hand. "But it's stopped now." He looked up at Will. "I won't be drinking again, Will. I promise you."

It was a supreme effort for Will to make himself nod. He breathed in deeply. "Okay." The word was a whisper, like wind cut by a kite string.

Those songs. Will didn't need to ask what song. He knew.

A seekrieger's song.

But which seekrieger? Calypso? Asia? Or someone else? Could one—or more—have survived the fire on the bay?

And what did they want now?

Will did the same thing he always did when he had questions that needed answers. He texted Angus.

"Welcome to the Evil Empire," Angus said with a grin as Will walked into the coffee shop. It was a franchise, just one more in a national chain, and the people of Walfang had expressed outrage when the owner had proposed opening it in the center of town. But it had opened anyway, and the summer people had flocked there, and five years later, it seemed as much of a landmark in Walfang as the town hall. Will usually avoided the place, though. There was good local coffee just up the street. Or he could get coffee strong enough to melt nails at Bella's. But Angus had said that he had some information about Carl, and suggested the place. Will was more than happy to meet in a location that felt anonymous. It was mostly empty at eight-thirty on a weeknight, and the people there were staring at laptops or reading, not paying attention to others around them or what was being said.

Angus took a sip from a tall, pink frothy drink topped with whipped cream. "Can you believe I'm drinking this girlie thing?"

Will sat down in the chair across from his. "Um— should I state the obvious?"

"No. Thanks for your restraint."

"It wasn't easy."

Angus liberated his long legs from beneath the small table between them, creating a tripping hazard for anyone who wanted to pass by. He took another sip of his enormous drink, pretending it absorbed his entire attention. "Are you going to get anything?" he asked, almost hopefully.

He doesn't want to tell me, Will realized. "I'm good."

"Listen . . ." Angus inhaled a heavy sigh. "I found out something about your uncle."

"Right." *Oh, God, do I want to hear the rest of this?*

"He was there the night Kirk Worstler's father died."

"What?"

"He was a witness." Will clamped his lips together and shook his head as Angus went on. "He saw Ezekiel Worstler jump out a window."

Will put his elbows on the table, ran his hands through his hair. "He was at the suicide."

"I talked to one of Barry's good buddies down at the station. A detective. He's been there a long time. I won't tell you who, but he pulled Carl's statement. I've got a copy." Angus pulled an envelope from his messenger bag. "Do you want it?"

Will looked at the manila envelope, wary. He thought of Pandora's box. Once the box was opened, the evil it contained could never be put back. "Why wouldn't he have told me?" Will asked.

"Maybe he didn't want to talk about it," Angus suggested. "Or maybe he thought you'd think he was crazy."

Will plucked the envelope from Angus's fingers. The statement was three pages, handwritten, hard to read, made even harder by a poor photocopy. Will scanned it, familiar with his uncle's uneven scrawl from eighteen years' worth of Christmas and birthday cards.

> The call came at 7:34 on Monday night, from the Mill Gallery. My security company had set up an alarm system there. I was on, so I went over.
>
> When I arrived, I saw that the front door was ajar—someone had smashed the glass and turned the knob. A brick was missing from the landscaped edge near the entrance, so I assumed someone had pried it free. When I stepped inside, I saw Ezekiel Worstler. He had his back to me, but when I called his name, he turned around. He had been slashing the paintings. I asked him what he was doing. Zeke and I had been in high school together, but I wasn't sure he recognized me. Something in his expression told me that he wasn't in his right mind. He'd always been a strange one. That family— well, [*words scratched out*].
>
> The Mill Gallery is built over a river, and there's a functioning water mill just outside. The gallery lit it up at night, and I could see it from the plate glass window, just behind where Zeke was standing.
>
> I was a little worried, since he had a knife, but I'd never known Zeke to be violent, so I didn't draw my gun. But he just grinned at me and turned back to the paintings. I said his name then, and he froze. He turned to me, and something in his face shifted. Just for a moment. "Carl

Archer?" he asked. I said his name again, and in a flash, he reached into his coat.

I did draw my gun then, but thank God I didn't fire, because what he pulled out was a flute. He played something on it—a little tune, no more than five or six notes—then tossed it aside. He let out a wild scream and came at me with the knife. I fired then, and the bullet hit him in the shoulder, but it didn't stop him. Zeke stabbed me in the arm, and I dropped the gun. I shouted his name again, and he backed away, then ran, headfirst, through the glass window.

I ran to the window, and I could see the splash where he had fallen—just at the place where the river is widest before it turns and reaches the sea. He surfaced for a moment, but said nothing. Then, I swear, I thought he was dragged down.

I waited for him to come back up, but he didn't.

I was about to turn away, when I saw a head surface out of the water. The edge of the lights caught her face. There was a woman down there—a young woman. Silver hair and eyes that almost glowed. She looked up at me with those eyes, and I felt terror like I'd never felt before. Then she grinned, and her teeth looked like they'd been filed to points.

I would know that face if I ever saw it again. A beautiful gargoyle, that's what she was.

Will put down the pages, feeling nauseated. Silver hair, glowing eyes—Will knew that description. That was Calypso—the seekrieger Gretchen had killed. Why had Ezekiel Worstler played the flute, then thrown himself out the window? That flute—Will had one that was similar. It was what seekriegers used to call to each other.

Angus had been right. After reading this, Will could completely understand why Carl wouldn't want to talk about it. He could also understand why Carl had started drinking. He'd eventually lost control of the security business, sold it to someone who had built it up to be one of the top employers in Walfang. But how could Carl have concentrated on work with Calypso's image in his mind? And he had said that he could hear her song sometimes. It would have been enough to make almost anyone crazy.

But Carl had said that he'd heard singing . . . recently. It was what made him take that drink.

Will tried to fit the pieces of the puzzle together in his mind but failed. Everything just fell apart. Calypso . . . Ezekiel . . . Gretchen . . . Asia . . . Kirk . . .

What does it mean?

The future seemed like a black hole, sucking in all light, all energy, taking everything into the void.

Angus leaned back in his chair and tossed his giant cup into the garbage. "What do you think?"

"I think the Worstlers are pretty messed up."

"I feel like all I ever do is deliver bad news that I don't even understand."

"What?"

"Nothing."

Will and Angus surveyed each other across the table, and Will found himself fighting the sense of unfamiliarity that had been plaguing him lately. It was as if he had woken up one day and realized that the world he lived in was populated by strangers. They looked the same, but he didn't know them anymore.

And even though Angus seemed mysterious to him, Will was sure that his friend was thinking the very same thought at the very same moment, and that was the strangest part of all.

Chapter Sixteen

Sea Witch's Lament (traditional)

*My sister, my sister, now lost in the
    sea,
With silvery hair and lips of ruby,
I never did love you in truth, hi de ho,
No, I never did love you in truth.*

*Though the waves and the tides both
    obey my command,
And I sink mighty ships with a wave
    of my hand,
You stole the one man that I loved,
    hi de ho,
Yes, you took the one man that I loved.*

*He spilled onto my island, a gift from
    the sea,
To lighten my loneliness with
    company,
But you breathed him away on a
    breeze, hi de ho,
Yes, you breathed him away on a
    breeze.*

*Yet he was unfaithful to you in the end,
And your heart was so broke that it
    never did mend,*

And your wrath was known better
   than you, hi de ho,
Yes, your wrath was known farther
   than you.

And none could escape the reach of
   your hate,
Even the powerful fell, soon or late.
Yes, I know that you'll send even me
   to my fate, hi de ho,
And I've nothing to do but to wait.

Will did not rise from his bed until well after eleven. He had woken at five and had heard the rain pattering against the windowsill, but had managed to go back to sleep. Now the clouds had blown through, and he could see blue sky beyond the red and yellow maple leaves outside his window.

He took a deep breath, trying to shake the ugly feeling that had settled over him last night and stayed with him through his dreams. He was still angry.

But why? Why?

Rationally, Will understood why Carl hadn't told him about Ezekiel Worstler. God, who would? It sounded crazy. Except that it didn't sound crazy. Perhaps because he'd been looking for signs of a seekrieger everywhere, evidence of mermaids and Sirens. Perhaps because he'd seen Gretchen set a body of water on fire.

It was as if the walls that had held the structure of his life, the boundaries of his existence, were melting away, or at the very least becoming less like walls and more like windows that allowed him to see new realities beyond.

The maple-sweet smell of his mother's baking still filled the house, and Will thought of all the mornings that he and Tim had sat together at the breakfast table, joking and laughing. Tim always liked to have sausages in the morning—"Meat for breakfast is manly," he'd said—and he would cook up an extra one for Will, which Will would then drown in syrup, much to his brother's delighted disgust.

His chest felt hollow, like an empty barrel. He missed his brother. He had lost so much—his dog, Asia—but losing his brother was like losing a leg. It was like losing part of himself.

Will pulled on his jeans and a faded old sweatshirt. He ran a hand through his shaggy hair and avoided the mirror. Shoving his feet into his shoes, he scuffed down the hall and clattered into the kitchen.

It was empty, so Will grabbed a muffin and sucked down a glass of milk in peace. He didn't want to admit how relieved he was not to see Gretchen. Will knew he owed her an apology, but he didn't think he could choke it out. Not yet. It was strange to be so close to someone—in proximity as well as emotionally—and yet to be overcome by your separateness.

Happiness is fleeting, he thought.

Will placed his dishes in the sink and walked out the back door. He stopped at the barn to feed the pygmy goats with their long, shaggy fur and strange eyes. Will spread some grain before the chickens and watched as they fought over the kernels. The rooster preened and strutted, too busy with his vanity to bother with the feed. Will aimed a few extra kernels in front of him. The rooster—with his glossy black feathers and long, gleaming green tail—amused him.

"You're an idiot," Will told the bird, who finally pecked at something. "But you've got it with the ladies."

Mud sucked at and clung to his sneakers as he went to the greenhouse to water the lettuce. His chores finished, Will headed back to the garage for his motorcycle. He cleaned off his shoes with a stick, then walked into the tidy space. His bike was reclining in a corner, and Will grabbed a helmet, then stroked the smooth leather of the seat. He remembered how Tim had helped him earn enough money for the bike. Whenever an odd job had come up—landscaping, grocery delivery, whatever—Tim would recommend his brother. And Tim had gone with him to help haggle over the bike. "Just let me do the talking," Tim had advised, and Will had, his heart hammering as his brother made an offer that was just a hair's breadth from being insulting. At one point Tim had threatened to walk on the whole negotiation, and Will had nearly screamed, "Wait! Wait!" but eventually the owner had come around. Tim had made sure Will got the bike at a price he could really afford, considering insurance and maintenance costs. It had been hard to trust him, but if he hadn't, Will wouldn't have the bike.

Jamming the helmet onto his head, Will kicked the bike to life. He roared out of the garage and rode up the road toward town. Even though Will was always careful behind the wheel of a car, he often drove fast on his motorcycle. He didn't know why. A few white clouds scudded across the sky, and a band of dark clouds—the rain from this morning—blocked the edge of the blue horizon.

Will parked at the marina and headed down to where his sailboat—the *Vagabond*—was moored. Tim's boat.

The water lapped gentle as a cat's tongue at the sides of the boat, and the *Vagabond* swayed slightly as he stepped aboard. He untied the rigging. The day had grown warm enough for Will to take off his sweatshirt, but the marina wasn't crowded. It was early October, after all, and the weekenders were finished for the year. He saw two boats under full sail out on the water, but both were coming in.

Will pulled up sail and turned the rudder starboard, guiding his boat through the narrow marina opening. It took only a few moments for him to reach the open water.

Will had always been a decent sailor. Nothing compared to his brother, of course, but he could manage a boat with ease. He remembered the scrappy "yacht club" Tim had helped put together when he was twelve. Tim, Will, Gretchen, and their two neighbors, Arnie and Jill, would meet at the tumbledown dock at the edge of the bay, at Arnie's house. Arnie and Jill were older—thirteen and fourteen—and each had access to family boats. Once Tim had actually organized a regatta. He'd challenged the kids at the Walfang Boating Club to a race. Those rich kids had been so surprised when they got to the "club" that they'd refused to race. But Tim talked them into it, implying— then outright stating—that a refusal to race meant a forfeit.

Naturally, they had raced.

Naturally, the rich kids won.

But Tim was undeterred. He was proudly enthusiastic about their efforts and talked eagerly of the next regatta. But then the summer ended, and the next year Jill and Arnie lost interest.

But Tim recalled those days with nothing but exuberance. He was proud that they had taken on the Boat Clubbers, as he called them. And in the retelling, Tim and Will always won the race.

Tim had loved the water.

Will looked out over the long horizon. It was impossible for Will to imagine heaven the way his Sunday school had taught him, angels and all that crap. But when he looked at the brilliant blue that dipped down to touch its darker shadow, he could imagine that Tim was somewhere on the other side. Will imagined him on a sandy shore, looking out. Watching, waiting for Will.

Maybe Asia was there, too.

Although when he thought of Asia, he thought of her still below the waves. He imagined her biding her time, living underwater, looking up at the light that filtered from above. He could almost see her brilliant green eyes glowing in the deep, her long dark hair floating around her like a cloud.

The sun had passed its height, and Will tacked to

port. In the distance, he could see a lighthouse on a rocky promontory. Regal houses stood guard along the sandy shore, their haughtiness daring anyone to come near. Tim had always dreamed of living in a beautiful house with a sea view.

"We live in a beautiful house with a sea view," Will would insist, but Tim just rolled his eyes.

"If you call that beautiful, I should be taking you to the optometrist. More like run-down. Oh, well. I guess we're keepin' it real."

Will had laughed. "Oh, it's real, all right."

It's real, all right.

Will lay back and closed his eyes, letting the small waves rock him. He tried to conjure an image of Tim and was alarmed to find that he couldn't quite do it. He caught a flash of dark hair, of laughing dark eyes, but what he got was a feeling more than a picture. He remembered what it was like to be with Tim, but the exact lines of his face, the curve of his jaw, the large hands, were fading.

Tim was disappearing from him, dissolving even in recollection.

Will had always taken for granted that Tim would be the other half of his memory. He would be there to recall the Christmases and the name of the doctor the time they'd had to go to the hospital because Tim had accidentally broken Will's nose in a brotherly wrestling match. He would be there to share stories about their parents when they were gone. But Tim had left him alone, the sole guardian of their shared history.

The boat jolted suddenly, and he opened his eyes.

A cloud had passed over the sun, and the sea had grown dark surprisingly fast. The cumulonimbi were rolling in quickly, and the water was choppy. Will hadn't gone far, but he would have to make it back to the marina quickly if he wanted to avoid the onset of the storm.

Cursing himself, Will tacked to starboard, heading back to the safety of the marina. Overhead, the clouds strove to close their dark curtain at the edge of the horizon as the breeze picked up, blowing the waves to whitecaps. The wind was in his favor, and the sails caught the breeze, the boat racing across the water. The rigging clips clinked, and overhead a single gull cried as she raced him to shore.

Dim through his damaged ear, Will heard the wind begin to rise, shrieking like a single note. The note rang on, growing louder, and a feeling of foreboding stole over Will.

He looked out to the edge of the dark horizon. There, small as a speck, was a figure—a human head half out of the water.

It's a buoy, he told himself, but he didn't believe it, and fear tore at him like a steel hook. A wave grew between him and the figure, and when it passed by, the seekrieger had disappeared.

The waves were growing wild, and Will raced to the mainmast. The *Vagabond* crawled up a tall wave, then plunged. A raindrop splattered his cheek, then one caught him in the eye, and in a moment it was raining fiercely, lashing him and the boat. Will had never seen a squall come on so quickly, although he had heard stories from fishermen and other boaters that it was possible. His heart pounded in his ears, and he felt as if he were pressed against a wall of panic, having the air squeezed from him.

The *Vagabond* tipped drunkenly as a rogue wave plowed into the port side. Will's feet slipped on the waxed wood surface, and he clung to the mast to stay aboard. He hauled himself to his feet, but a moment later another wave dealt a punishing blow. The boat tipped and capsized.

Will dove into the water, trying to avoid the timber. With the wild weather, he had to be careful to avoid a head injury.

When he came up, the rain lashed at him like a beast unleashed. He only had time to gulp a mouthful of oxygen before being smacked with a merciless wall of water. He struggled toward the surface, but couldn't seem to work his way into the open air. His chest felt tight, he needed to breathe—

Something grabbed his shoulder, and bubbles burst from his mouth in a silent scream. It was the thing. The seekrieger. The dark thoughts of his dead brother had called her to him.

He kicked and struggled as he felt himself being pulled up, up by an iron arm. He was still fighting as they broke through the surface, screaming as the waves assaulted them.

"Will!" In his delirium, Will imagined that the thing was calling him by name. The grip encased him so that he was completely paralyzed.

"Will!" the creature said again, this time distinctly. "Will, stop."

And the voice did make him stop. Anyone would have stopped for the rich, velvet texture, the sweet tones as clear as a silver bell. But Will stopped because he recognized the voice.

There, before him, were a pair of brilliant green eyes. Porcelain skin, long dark hair.

The seekrieger was Asia.

Chapter Seventeen

From The Eumenides, *by Aeschylus*

Blow forth on him the breath of
 wrath and blood,
Scorch him with reek of fire that
 burns in you,
Waste him with new pursuit—swift,
 hound him down!

A branch scraped against the window, pressing inward like an unwelcome neighbor. The sun had winked out behind the dark clouds, and even the barn, which was not twenty paces from the house, disappeared in the driving rain. It was late afternoon, and Gretchen was making herself a cup of tea. The gloomy chill had begun to sink into her bones, but she felt safe in the cozy kitchen.

The Archer kitchen was different from her own. One entire wall was given over to hooks that held cast-iron pots and pans. Stoneware jugs held a motley collection of spatulas, ladles, and wooden spoons. The Archer house was old and drafty and in places felt in need of repair, but the kitchen was airy and modern, with a top-of-the-line commercial oven for Mrs. Archer's work. The sink was a vintage 1930s enamelware with two basins and a built-in drying rack—the same sink that Mr. Archer's grandmother had installed. The enamel had partially worn away in one spot near the drain, and Gretchen loved the gritty slate texture revealed underneath. The long farm table, too, dated from the time of Mr. Archer's grand-parents. Made of heavy oak, it felt solid and perma-nent beneath Gretchen's spread palms. There were scars in the wood from years of use, a deep gouge from a foolish moment when Tim and Will had placed a heavy air-conditioning unit on the surface, but it was still beautiful. Mr. Archer had torn up the ugly linoleum that his parents had added and unearthed wide pine planks, which he'd sanded and refinished, and which now shone up at Gretchen with a cheerful brownish yellow. In many ways, this was Gretchen's ideal kitchen, just as Will's family was the ideal fam-ily. Or had been, until Tim died.

Rain thrummed against the window, driven almost sideways by the wind. Bananas was still asleep on her bed, curled atop her pillow, happily oblivious to the storm that raged outside. Johnny had gone to record something at the studio in Montauk, and Mr. and Mrs. Archer had an appointment with a supplier in town. She didn't know where Will was, and it didn't occur to her to worry about him. It was only four o'clock. She assumed everyone would be home within an hour or so, as Mrs. Archer usually served dinner at six.

The Archers kept their house cooler than Gretchen was used to, but she was wearing her new wool socks and feeling rather cozy when the door burst open without warning and there stood Will, dripping and blue-lipped, pale as death. Gretchen nearly screamed, but then someone appeared behind him, as tall as he, and also soaked to the bone.

Asia stepped through the back door and into the kitchen, like a creature crossing from one dimension into another, and Gretchen dropped her mug. It shattered across the floor, sending shards of wet porcelain under the cupboards.

Everyone was still; nobody knew what to say.

They might have stayed that way forever, still as statues, turned to stone, but Bananas chose that moment to strut in. She took one look at Will and darted into the living room.

"You're not dead," Gretchen said to Asia. Emotions whipped through her at dizzying speed: fear, relief, joy, dread, confusion, envy. Yes, envy, for there was Asia, looking even more beautiful than Gretchen remembered, standing beside Will. Gretchen called in an instant all of the jealousy she'd felt surrounding Asia, the fear she'd had that Will had been falling in love with her. And here she was—alive.

"I know," Asia said.

Will walked to the counter and grabbed some paper towels, then began gathering up the broken crockery.

"You're making it worse," Gretchen said as Will wiped up the spill, shedding his own water all over the floor. "Leave it. You need to dry off."

Will stood up with a sigh. He looked at Asia. "You can borrow some of my stuff," he told her. He reached under the sink and grabbed three ragged old towels that they'd used to dry Guernsey after her baths. Asia and Will rubbed themselves off, and he motioned for her to follow him up the stairs.

They disappeared, leaving Gretchen alone with her confusion. She didn't know what to think, so she busied herself with cleaning up the broken cup, gathering the large pieces and placing them in the trash, mopping up the smaller ones with paper towels. She took the old towels that Will had dropped on the floor and dumped them into the hamper in her room. Then she grabbed the mop and ran it over the wooden planks. When she had finished, she put the mop away and went to sit on the couch in the living room. Bananas padded her way over to Gretchen's lap, then curled up comfortably.

Will appeared first, barefoot and in fresh jeans and a long-sleeved T-shirt. His hair was uncombed but had been rubbed dry. It was slicked away from his face, and Gretchen was surprised by the full view of his scar, which was usually obscured by a curtain of hair.

He sat down across from her, perched on one of the horribly uncomfortable chairs. He leaned forward and looked into Gretchen's face so seriously that she squirmed. Bananas raised her head and gave Gretchen a reproachful look, then went back to dreaming. "We saved the boat," Will announced, as if Gretchen had any idea what he meant.

"What?"

He thought a moment and started over. "Asia's come to help us," Will said, and that one sentence sent a dagger of anger through Gretchen's heart. A moment before, her confusion had been giving way to relief . . . but now she felt intense mistrust.

"Why?" Gretchen snapped, just as Asia appeared in the doorway.

She was dressed in Will's jeans and a blue-and-white button-down shirt, her black hair raked into damp rows. The clothes were baggy on her, but somehow she made them look elegant. "You're in danger, Gretchen," Asia said. Her voice was gentle, compassionate, and Gretchen felt the anger melt away. "But surely you know that."

Gretchen shook her head. "It's too much."

"I know."

"Let me just get used to seeing you."

"Okay." Asia turned, and Gretchen could see that her damp hair was making her shirt cling to her back. Asia disappeared into the kitchen, and Will put his head in his hands. Seconds ticked by in silence.

Asia reappeared carrying a glass of water, which she handed to Gretchen. Three deep gulps and Gretchen felt better. Asia sat down in the chair beside Will's and looked at Gretchen steadily.

Gretchen didn't know how to phrase her question politely. Finally, she just blurted, "Why aren't you dead?"

"In a way, I am."

"Don't talk to me in riddles, okay? Things are confusing enough." Gretchen looked at Will, whose head was still down. He had heard the story already, she supposed.

"It was no ordinary fire," Asia countered. "The fire

of vengeance burned through us, Gretchen, but it didn't destroy our bodies. It destroyed our immortality."

"You mean those things are still out there?" Gretchen whispered.

"Out there—under a death sentence. As am I. But they are not likely to come here. Calypso and her band have spent thousands of years in the water. They can't walk among humans as easily as I can." Asia looked outside, where the rain was starting to ease. The dark clouds had turned to pale gray. Two birds sang their approval. "Still, I suppose I should be grateful. In a way, you saved me."

"What? How?"

"You know that I was unable to break a promise, unable to lie. But I did break a promise—the promise to deliver you to Calypso."

"Deliver me?" Gretchen barely dared to breathe. She stared at Will. "I think there's something you for-got to tell me."

Will's face burned, and he stared at the floor. "She couldn't do it." He looked up at Gretchen. "She tried to save you."

"*After* she tried to kill me?"

"I was bound to Calypso by a promise I made years ago. A promise I was forced to make, to save the life of someone I cared for," Asia explained.

"I thought you had died for me," Gretchen cried. "Do you know what that feels like?"

"I would have," Asia said. "I thought I was going to. That—or worse. The penalty if I did not deliver you was that I would turn into a zombie."

Gretchen paused a moment to take this in. "You don't look like a zombie to me."

"No. Because your fire made me mortal. If that hadn't happened, I would have become . . . something else."

"How do you know you're mortal?"

Asia smiled, shrugged. "My strength is weakened. And—for the first time—I know what fear feels like."

Gretchen sighed, feeling the anger again seep out of her slowly. She knew what it was like to be in an impossible situation. That was something she and Asia had in common. "I'm sorry."

"It isn't for you to feel sorry for me. That was a decision I made."

Gretchen covered her face with her hands. "I can't believe I killed them."

"It had to happen, Gretchen," Asia said gently. "The universe exists in delicate balance, and has been struggling to blot out the darkness the seekriegers created from the beginning. The Fury, Tisiphone, pursued them for many years. Over the ages. She is one of three sisters, the Eumenides. She is the one who avenges murder, and she left the underworld and was born into human form to stop them."

"Tisiphone." Gretchen heard the word with a shade of recognition, and wondered if she had read about the Fury in a textbook somewhere. "From the underworld."

"Every five hundred years, Tisiphone is consumed in fire and reborn," Asia explained. "Like a phoenix. From the ashes of destruction comes new life. And now, Will tells me, you have both been having accidents. That things have been happening—a dog attack, a mugging—that are beyond your explanation."

Gretchen remembered the face in the waterspout.

Gretchen's mind was swimming, struggling to put the pieces together. Will raised his head. He looked at her with a mixture of expectancy and fear. "So is Tisiphone angry that I killed the Sirens before she did?" Gretchen asked. "Is that why she's after me—after Will and me?"

"After you?" Asia cocked her head. "I'm sorry, Gretchen, you've misunderstood me."

Gretchen nodded, but the fog in her mind only thickened. She couldn't tell if it was the mental strain or simply the melody of Asia's voice that made her want to curl up in a ball and fall asleep, forget the world right there on the couch. But she forced herself to pay attention, to watch Asia's lips as she formed the words.

"Tisiphone doesn't want to kill you," Asia said. "Tisiphone *is* you."

The rain fell, light and steady, dampening Gretchen's hair, collecting heavily on her eyelashes, like tears. Her new sneakers slogged through the wet grass, picking up green clippings and mud. A light October chill hung in the air, but it wasn't unpleasant. The clouds had lifted, and the late-afternoon sun was making a reluctant appearance.

She was walking toward the bay.

Gretchen didn't know why. Maybe she wanted to look out over open space. Maybe she needed to see the scene of her crime. Of Tisiphone's crime.

Tisiphone is you.

No, she thought. *No. I'm Gretchen. I'm Gretchen and no one else.*

But that thought was followed closely by another: *Who were you when that mugger attacked you?*

She had felt something come over her then, almost as if she had surrendered herself to someone else. And when she set the bay on fire—she had become someone else then, too. Every time the fire burned through her, it was as if she was channeling someone's power.

But why? Why me?

She thought of her mother then—the woman she had grown up thinking of as her mother, Yvonne. She had always treated Gretchen with a certain measure of restraint, almost fear. Gretchen remembered one morning when she was small and had padded softly into her parents' bedroom. Yvonne was sleeping on her stomach, her lips slightly parted. Dark hair splashed across the pale green pillowcase. The blue and green duvet was pulled up around her, like a cloud, or a wave. Gretchen thought she looked like a sleeping angel. She touched her mother's arm gently, to wake her. Yvonne had woken with a start—shot up in bed. She stared at Gretchen with wide eyes, as if her daughter had stepped directly out of Yvonne's nightmare.

"Mama?" Gretchen said.

Yvonne started to shake her head then, but her movements had woken Johnny, who grinned sleepily. "Hey, sugar bunny," he said happily.

Gretchen walked around the bed and stepped into his arms, her heart pounding, as if she had caught her mother's fear, like a cold. But her father's warm arms brought her back to life, and by the time he released her, Yvonne had recovered. She was even smiling, laughing, suggesting pancakes, like any regular Saturday morning.

Gretchen didn't think her mother knew the truth—how could she? But she had suspected something. What had Mafer said? *We know things about people.* Perhaps Yvonne had known but not known, and that was what kept her from loving Gretchen the way a mother should. The way Gretchen had always wanted.

The tears came then, flowing fast, mingling with the rain that had wet her cheeks. She supposed that there were people in the world who might be happy to learn that they had amazing powers. She could hear Angus joking: "Dude, you're a superhero!"

But she had never asked to be a superhero. And she had a dark premonition that it involved sacrifices she wasn't prepared to make.

I just want to be Gretchen, that's all.

Her clothes were growing heavy with water as she climbed the small hill that bordered the bay. Sun filtered through the clouds in thick shafts, cutting the gray with buttery yellow. The water was calm but dappled, like a sheet of old glass. In the distance, the green shrubbery that topped the cliffs had turned dark in the dreary light. It was as if the color had drained out of the scene, all except for the columns of light that shone down on the water.

Footsteps approached from behind her.

Gretchen had supposed that Will would follow her, so she was surprised when Asia's voice said, "I suspected you would come here."

Gretchen looked out over the level water, trying to imagine the surface as it burned, the anguished cries of the seekriegers as they suffered and died. "I don't want to be an executioner," Gretchen said.

"We can't always choose what we are," Asia replied. Her voice was even, but also sad.

Gretchen turned to face her. Asia's green eyes held her gaze, and Gretchen wondered how she felt to be a Siren. Even though she was mortal now, she was far from human. Had she ever wished she were? Perhaps not. After all, she wasn't like Gretchen. She hadn't thought herself to be one thing and then discovered she was something else.

"I was found in the ashes," Gretchen said, the thought just occurring to her. "My mother died in a fire."

Asia looked out at the columns of light. They were so thick they gave the illusion of holding up the sky. "Your mother was consumed in that fire. She died, and was reborn. As you."

"You're saying that I have no mother. Or—that I am my own mother?"

Asia shrugged. "Tisiphone has no beginning, and no end. At least, not one that I know of. She—you— have existed longer than any of my kind."

Gretchen felt as if the picture being painted for her kept shifting and morphing, taking on new shape and meaning the harder she looked. "What about me—Gretchen?"

Her voice sounded thin, almost whiny to her ears, and she hated it.

"Every incarnation of Tisiphone is different," Asia told her. "You are you and you are her. Your strength lies in both of you." Asia touched Gretchen's hand gently. "You are Gretchen. But you are also a Fury."

"No," Gretchen whispered, shaking her head slowly. "That's not what I am."

Asia nodded and looked out at the clouds again. The rain had stopped completely, and the clouds were breaking into fat clumps, allowing the sky to show through in bits and pieces. The shapes shifted slowly as they moved across the sky, refusing to be defined in space.

"Not yet. Not fully," Asia agreed. "Tisiphone is what you are becoming. That was why Calypso wanted me to deliver you before you awakened. While you were still at your weakest."

Asia turned her head, as if she heard something. "Will is calling for you," she said, a moment before Gretchen heard the distant shout. She heard it again, and Will appeared, running toward them. He had a cell phone in his hand. His hair was dry now, but his feet were still bare, which told Gretchen that whatever he had come to tell them, the news was bad.

Her heart felt as if it had shrunk, constricting the flow of the blood through her body. *I don't want to hear it,* she thought, but she couldn't stop him from coming toward them, couldn't stop the news from being what it was. She felt like a stick borne forward on a swiftly flowing river, powerless to change course, following a route worn into rock over ages, as changeless as the march of time.

"Gretchen!" Will raced toward her. "I just talked to Angus." He was breathless, his face flushed. He looked beautiful and terrified. "Kirk is freaking out."

"What?"

"He's at the diner, totally flipping. He's got a knife and is threatening to kill himself, but he's demanding to talk to you." Will's body was tensed; he looked ready to take flight.

Gretchen clung to Asia's arm, and the seekrieger placed a strong arm around her waist, supporting her. To her shame, Gretchen's first reaction was anger. She didn't want to go help Kirk. She had other problems to deal with. She didn't need to handle Kirk's drama right now.

But he was at Bella's—with a knife. Anger gave way to guilt. *I'm responsible for the fact that he's there,* she realized. An image of Kirk's sad, frightened eyes flashed in her mind. Compassion overwhelmed her.

"We have to go now," Asia said.

"Yes," Gretchen agreed.

At once they ran, together, racing back across the field. With every step, Gretchen felt herself driven forward, toward a destiny that she wasn't sure she wanted but didn't think she could avoid.

Chapter Eighteen

From A Cultural Study of Madness,
by Philip de Guerre, PhD

Many cultures hold beliefs in spirit, or demonic, possession, and it is mentioned specifically at several points in the Bible, as well as other sacred texts. We now know, of course, that spirit possession unequivocally does not exist—the symptoms ascribed to those "possessed" mirror accounts of people with several different kinds of mental illness or psychiatric disorders, including Tourette's syndrome, bipolar disorder, psychosis, multiple personality disorder, and so on. As you see, society finds a way to label different types of "abnormal" or dissociative behavior, often endowing these people with powers beyond those of mere mortals.

Angus was waiting by the back entrance, hunched into a navy peacoat, when Will screeched to a stop in the parking lot. He slammed Carl's truck into park and yanked open the door. Gretchen was already out the other side, Asia spilling onto the asphalt behind her.

"That kid is so fired," Angus said as Gretchen brushed past him and into the diner.

The first face Gretchen saw was Angel's. His jaw

was slack, his complexion ashy—Angel, whose first response was always rage, looked sick and frightened. Lisette was parked at the doorway to the dining room, making sure that no customers tried to intervene. Kirk was on the floor, writhing and singing in a language that Gretchen didn't know. The words were harsh and guttural, strange and ugly to her ear. In his hand was a boning knife, and there was blood on his sleeve and a bloody handprint on his white apron. Dark red drops splattered and smeared the white tiles, as if he had half dragged himself across the floor, beneath the metal prep table.

"Kirk," Gretchen called softly.

His head snapped toward her, and for a moment he smiled softly, gratefully, like he was really Kirk, and was really happy to see her. Then the expression darkened, and a strange fire came into the dark pools of his eyes. He sang a few more words, then—with an awkward, contorting gesture—plunged the boning knife into his thigh.

Will gasped. "Jesus, Kirk!"

"Oh shit!" Angus pulled out his cell phone and started to dial emergency services. Asia grabbed the phone out of his hand and tossed it into the sink, where it landed with a metal clang. "I just bought that!" Angus protested, then withered a little under Asia's glare.

Kirk yanked the knife out of his thigh and scrambled to his feet. With a shout, he plunged toward Gretchen, knife high. Gretchen pulled up her arm to defend herself, but Asia was faster. She caught Kirk's wrist and twisted it, but his fingers clung to the handle of the blade like a vine grown tight around a branch.

"I'll destroy this body before I let you harm her," Asia said.

Kirk started at the voice, as if Asia's face had no relevance but the voice had stirred a distant memory. He stared up at Asia, and his eyes glittered with a fierce golden light. For the first time, Gretchen was certain that whatever that thing was, it wasn't Kirk. "Asia," the thing said with a strange inflection. "Are you going to protect her?" The voice was sneering, and a hungry light illuminated his face, as if this thing would relish such a challenge. "Destroy this body, then. I dare you."

Asia narrowed her eyes and looked as if she just might, but Gretchen shouted, "No!"

In the moment of uncertainty, Kirk broke free, but he did not lunge toward Gretchen. Instead, he backed into the table and raised his arm.

Gretchen leaped at him before he could plunge the knife into his own chest. The blade caught her on the shoulder, opening a wound that bled onto her new peach shirt.

And suddenly everyone was in motion. Angel, Will, Angus, Asia—everyone lunged forward and pinned Kirk, still screaming, to the floor. But something had changed. He was screaming in English. His voice was hysterical, but it had lost its strange inflection, its guttural cast. His eyes remained dark pools as Asia pinned his arm to the table, and he dropped the knife to the floor, where it clattered and spun.

"Why did you stop me?" he screamed. "You shouldn't have stopped me!"

Asia whispered something in his ear. He screamed again, but she whispered more, until finally he gave up shouting and started coughing. After a moment, his body relaxed a little, and his eyes fluttered closed.

The room had grown completely silent, and it took Gretchen a moment to realize that Kirk had actually fallen asleep. He was splayed backward across a metal table, limbs twisted at odd angles, blood flowing from the wound in his leg, and he was sleeping sound as a baby.

Asia cradled Kirk in her arms and placed him gently on the table.

"Oh, Asia," Lisette breathed.

Angel looked at Asia. "I had a whole speech prepared for if I ever saw you again. It's about how pissed I was that you bailed out on us at the end of the summer, but I think I'll skip it."

Will touched Gretchen's shoulder with a finger. "This looks bad."

"It hardly hurts." Gretchen winced slightly as she twisted her shoulder, trying to get a better look at the injury.

Angus fished his cell phone out of the sink. "It's still working," he announced. "I know you were all really concerned. I'm dialing 911 now."

"He'll be all right," Asia said, looking down at Kirk.

"That dude needs to be in a mental hospital," Angus said. "He's completely out of control."

"He's been doing so well." Angel surprised Gretchen with the sadness in his voice.

"What happened?" Lisette asked. "Nothing seemed to provoke him. One minute he was Kirk; the next minute he was—"

"Someone else," Gretchen finished for her.

Lisette nodded. "It was like that."

Angel took her hand, and they both looked down at the sleeping Kirk as if he were their baby.

Asia gave Gretchen a knowing look. "He was not himself," she said.

"So who was he?" Angus asked. He sounded like he was joking, but Gretchen suspected that he wasn't.

Asia looked at him as if she might say something, then thought better of it. "We need to get Kirk to the hospital," she said, just as red lights began to flicker through the window.

"He's a frequent guest there, anyway," Will said.

Asia didn't reply. She simply brushed Kirk's dark hair away from his damp forehead. In a moment an EMT in dark blue stepped in, carrying a bag of equipment. He took one look at Kirk and walked over to the table asking, "Anyone else?"

"Take care of him first," Gretchen said as the man's partner came in.

"Let me take a look," the new EMT insisted.

Gretchen pulled back her sleeve. The EMT frowned. "Pull it back further, please." She did, twisting so that the rear of her shoulder showed. He inspected her shoulder, then gave her a wry smile. "No wound," he said.

"What?"

"Must be the other guy's blood."

Gretchen twisted her neck to get a better view as both EMTs turned to Kirk. She had felt the knife slice her flesh. But he was right—there was no wound.

Kirk wasn't in any danger, but he needed to go to the hospital for his leg.

"I'll ride with him in the ambulance," Asia offered.

Will, Gretchen, and Angus decided to follow in the truck, while Lisette and Angel had to stay and clean up. Angus called Kirk's sister to let her know what was happening.

"Great to see you again, Asia, by the way," Angus said as Will took Gretchen's arm and led her toward the door. "Glad you showed up. Things were just getting a little boring around here."

"Would someone fill this out?" the triage nurse asked. She looked at Gretchen through round horn-rimmed glasses and passed a stack of papers across the desk. Gretchen took the paperwork and followed Will into the waiting room. Angus was sitting there, munching popcorn and staring at a television blaring a game show. He looked over at them and poured the rest of the popcorn into his mouth before tossing the black bag into the trash. Then he brushed the crumbs off his lap and hurried over to them.

"Everything okay?" he asked.

"Yeah," Gretchen told him.

"Where's Asia?" Will asked.

Gretchen understood that it was perfectly natural for him to ask, but it still irritated her. She didn't like to hear Asia's name on his lips. It sounded too natural there, too beautiful.

"She's with Kirk," Angus said, and then—as if she'd heard them talking about her—Asia appeared. Her movements were slow and she seemed thoughtful as she walked up to them.

"How is he?" Will asked.

"He's surprisingly strong." Asia frowned. "Not many survive what he's been through."

"Yeah, about that," Angus put in. "Would anyone like to fill me in on just what that is?"

Asia cocked her head, as if she had just noticed Angus. "Why are you even here?"

He rolled his eyes. "Lady, I have no idea."

"I want him to stay," Gretchen announced. Will lifted his eyebrows slightly, but she ignored him.

"Seriously?" Angus looked delighted.

"Look, why don't you just tell us what's going on?" Gretchen demanded. She glared at Asia. Her body was shaking with the effort it took not to strike out, hit something. "You're the only one who knows, so just—share."

Asia looked around the waiting room. It was empty. Nine twenty-three on a Sunday night, and people seemed to be avoiding injuring themselves. The triage nurse sat behind her counter, chatting on the phone with someone who—by the tone and content of the conversation—seemed to be her daughter. She wasn't likely to eavesdrop on them. Asia gestured for the others to follow, and she led them to the far corner, over by the windows. Asia perched herself on the edge of one of the tasteful but uncomfortable blue chairs. A ficus sat behind her, sad in its leafy attempt to make the setting seem less depressing.

Gretchen took the chair next to Asia, and Will sat on the other side of Gretchen. Angus flopped into a chair across from them. He was the only one who looked eager to hear what she had to say. Gretchen thought that Will looked exactly how she was feeling—filled with dread.

Asia pressed her palms against her knees, then took a deep breath. "You know about spirit possession, I suppose?" She looked up.

"Totally saw *The Exorcist*," Angus said with a wave, like he was an expert.

Asia looked at him a moment, then turned to Gretchen and Will.

"Is that what happened to Kirk?" Gretchen asked. "He was possessed by a demon?"

Asia flinched at the word *demon*, but eventually she nodded. "Not a demon exactly, but—"

"Not *not* a demon," Will finished for her.

A humorless smile touched Asia's lips. "It's probably the right word. The only word."

"Does the demon have a name?" Gretchen asked.

"Circe," Asia said, touching the smooth wooden

arm of the chair. "She's a very powerful witch. She was sent to dwell in the spirit world, but something has awakened her."

"Something like . . . ?" Gretchen prompted.

"Like the change in her sister and rival."

"Circe is a Siren?"

"Her mother was one of our kind—Perse—and her father another immortal. There is Siren in her, but she is more powerful than we are. Much more. Still, somehow Calypso sent Circe to the spirit world. Now that Calypso is diminished, Circe has resurfaced. The destruction of many Sirens has given those who dwell on the next plane new strength. The universe is woven together in a web, Gretchen—the human world, the spirit world. You cannot disturb one strand without affecting the fabric. The spirit world is reacting to the shock waves from this world."

Gretchen glanced over at Will, who looked pale but calm, as if he had a new understanding of something. "So—the dead are gaining power?"

Asia nodded. "For now."

"What does she want?" Will asked. That was one thing Gretchen loved about him—his directness, his eagerness to get to the point.

"She has one foot in our world and one foot in the Beyond. She wants to cross over fully, to regain her power." Asia's green eyes drifted over Gretchen's shoulder, as if she were trying to focus on something in the Beyond—something she couldn't quite see. "And for that, she wants to possess Gretchen. Or kill her."

Gretchen closed her eyes, feeling a heavy weight descending over her limbs. She wasn't surprised by this statement at all.

"Kill her?" Will demanded. "Why would she want to kill her?"

"If she kills her, Tisiphone will be reborn in flame. But that moment between life and death—"

"That's when she could possess me," Gretchen finished.

"She can take the shape of wind, mist, vapor. She's been gaining power slowly. First she inhabited a dog. Then a criminal. Then Kirk . . ."

"So—she was in Kirk? That's what you're saying?" Will demanded. "But then why did he try to stab himself in the heart? It doesn't make sense."

"Kirk is stronger than she guessed, I suppose," Asia said. "He thought that if he could kill himself, he would be rid of her. But by the time he had the strength—the mental strength—to try, she had already departed his body."

"So he would have killed himself for nothing." Gretchen shuddered at the thought that Kirk would have sacrificed himself. *Would I have done the same?* she wondered.

"Circe can affect the minds of those around her," Asia went on. "When Odysseus arrived on her island, she turned his men into pigs. Not literally into pigs, of course, although that is how the story is told. She simply magnified the worst aspects of their personalities until they were no better than pigs, wallowing in their own muck, searching greedily for their next meal."

"What does that have to do with Gretchen?" Will asked.

"She is the Fury. If Circe can kill her, she will obtain her powers. And if she strikes now, while Gretchen's powers are in a weakened state, she may succeed."

"What powers?" Angus asked. He was grinning, as if he had just stumbled in on an elaborate joke.

Nobody spoke. Nobody even looked at him.

"What powers?" Angus repeated. But this time his voice was faint, as if he was only now beginning to realize the seriousness of the situation. "Do you mean . . . are we talking about the fire stuff?"

Will looked at him sharply.

"I don't have any powers," Gretchen snapped.

Asia leaned forward. "You can be stabbed but not killed. The only way for you to die is by drowning—or being consumed by your own flame, which happens only once every five hundred years, at the end of your life cycle. And you could set this entire hospital complex on fire with your mind."

"No, I couldn't. And even if I could, I wouldn't want to. Why would I?" Her voice was almost pleading, and Will tightened his grip on her fingers.

"If she can't be killed, then why does Circe keep attacking?"

"She hopes to weaken Gretchen enough so that she can possess her mind," Asia explained. "Fear can do that. Pain can do it. If she can't accomplish that, she will drown you."

"I never asked for this," Gretchen whispered.

"None of us ask for the gifts we are given," Asia replied.

"But it doesn't really matter, does it?" Will asked. "I mean, what good is fire against mist? How do you destroy something like that?"

"I don't know," Asia admitted. Her eyes never left Gretchen's. "All I know is that she won't stop until she destroys you."

Gretchen let her gaze drop to the floor. "I won't fight her," she said, lifting her eyes.

Asia and Gretchen regarded each other for a long moment. Gretchen felt as if she were reaching out to Asia over miles, or maybe across dimensions. Like it or not, Gretchen had more in common with this Siren than she did with Will. Asia was truly the only one who could understand what it was like to be a stranger among humans, an outsider.

"It's your choice, of course," Asia replied. "But you must understand that if you do not stop her, many will suffer. And you will die."

Gretchen hung her head. Kill or be killed—what kind of choice was that? She had nothing to say.

Really, there was no choice at all.

Chapter Nineteen

*Sparks flew up as the pyre ignited—
those were the fireflies she had seen
before. Heat seared through her: agony
tore at her flesh in a lightning flash. And
then she felt her flesh vibrating,
humming with energy.*

*The angry faces of the mob had
turned to shock and then—fear.*

*Gretchen realized that her wrists
were no longer bound. She lifted her
arms and looked down to see them lined
with flaming feathers.*

Still she burned on. . . .

She awoke, disoriented, to faded rose-patterned wall-paper. A strange room, a chipped white bureau with glass knobs, lace curtains yellowed with age, a blue-and-white-striped easy chair that sat, resigned and lumpy, in the corner. Her mind scrambled for a moment, as if skidding across a sheet of ice, then finally found a toehold: the sweet smell of her pillowcase reminded her of Will. She was in the Archers' guest room.

The window beyond the yellowed lace was dark, although the glowing green numbers on the clock beside her bed read 6:30. *It should be lighter,* she thought, a moment later registering the soft patter of rain.

She caught the damp, dreamy smell of wet leaves, and Gretchen realized that she had left the window slightly open; raindrops splattered against the white windowsill. Gretchen sighed, reluctant to leave the cozy cave of her blankets. A chill had settled over her room, lying across her bedspread like frost.

Gretchen tucked her knees to her chest as guilt crept over her. The image of Kirk stole into her mind, and she felt stricken. Trembling, tears streamed down, dripping over the bridge of her nose and wetting her pillow. Outside, a sparrow chirped, then fell silent, discouraged by the rain.

Gretchen was just wondering how she could possibly get out of bed when she heard a crash from the room beside hers, then a muffled curse. Her room was right off the kitchen—Mrs. Archer was probably baking.

Gretchen squeezed her eyes shut, but she knew that sleep was impossible. *I don't want this life,* she thought.

But there was no use pitying herself; she knew that. It was strange. Thinking of Tim here, in the Archer house, didn't hurt her as much as it did elsewhere. The whole house was filled with him. His red and black plaid jacket still hung in the front closet; a photo of him and Will ages nine and seven was on the side table in the living room; even the small plate— ugly and misshapen, but cheerful in yellow—where Mrs. Archer placed her used teabags was a relic from one of Tim's summer camps.

I'm lucky. The thought surprised her, and a moment later the sweet vanilla scent of baking scones crept under her blanket. *I am lucky,* she realized, *to be here with Will's family. To have Will, who cares about me. To have had Tim in my life. In spite of everything, I'm lucky. Not everyone has that.* And she thought of Kirk and his sister, who didn't understand him, and his mother, who never thought about him at all.

Outside, the rain drummed on. She swung her legs from beneath the blanket, placed her bare feet onto the wide painted boards, and stood up. A deep breath, and she wiped the tears from her eyes. She shut the window, silencing the rain, then pulled her fleece from beneath her pillow and yanked on some new, soft socks. Then she padded into the kitchen to help Mrs. Archer.

Later that afternoon, Gretchen lay on her back looking up at the sky through the filter of leaves. Light poured in through the irregular patchwork of scallop-edged ovals, illuminating the yellow and orange with a soft glow. A light breeze lifted a leaf and it parachuted in an uneven zigzag, finally landing on Gretchen's neck. The air was pungent with the smell of decay and wood smoke from the fireplace at Will's house. Overhead, strips of white clouds sat on a blue sky, as if they had no intention of going anywhere.

She stretched out, pressing the bottom of her feet against the tree's trunk. Her hair was spread across a carpet of moss, grass, and fallen leaves and a small twig dug into her shoulder blade, but Gretchen didn't mind it. She had lain beneath this tree countless times, looking up through the tall branches that cascaded to the ground around her, forming a natural curtain that hid her, and a faded red canoe, from sight. "The fairy place," she had called it the first time Will had showed it to her, when they were five years old. Tim was old enough to reject that as the name, so Gretchen and Will were careful to call it just "the tree" in front of him. But in her heart, Gretchen had always thought the place was magical.

The leaves rustled slightly and the curtain parted. "I knew I'd find you here," Will said. He hesitated, as if waiting for an invitation to come inside.

Gretchen didn't offer one. She just kept looking up at the distant sky.

Finally Will gave up waiting and came to sit beside her. The yellow canopy was enormous—it offered more than enough room for the boat and three or four people to stand or sit. Will sat down, half-lotus, beside Gretchen. He picked up a leaf and twisted the yellow stem. Then he looked up at the sky. Gretchen wondered what he saw there.

They sat that way for a long time, just looking at the leaves and the vast blue expanse beyond. In the distance, Gretchen could hear the high-pitched drone of a leaf blower. A bird trilled once, twice, and fell silent. A truck rumbled and rattled by on the road.

People were thinking of pumpkins and hot cider, apples and squash. Normal life.

Gretchen had always loved fall in New York City, but it was even more beautiful here. In Manhattan, she would take a walk through Central Park to remind herself of the steady change that was going on, the progression from heat to cold reflected in the fading leaves. But she hadn't been surrounded by the change the way she was out here. In a way, being in Walfang helped her feel like a part of it, as if the change was occurring not only all around her but within her as well.

And she *was* changing. Or, perhaps, not changing. More like realizing that she wasn't what she thought she was. The world around her was falling asleep, and she was waking up.

"How is this going to turn out well?" Gretchen asked.

Will didn't answer, and she rolled over to look at him. She propped her head on her hand. "I mean, forget the whole Circe thing. Just forget that for a minute. Even without that, I'm this . . . *thing* now."

"You're the same," Will said, but he was looking at the leaf caught in his fingers, not at her.

"I just want to be normal." An old movie line echoed in Gretchen's mind. "I want to be a real girl."

Will smiled wryly. "Well, it worked out for Pinocchio."

Gretchen laughed, but it was so weak that it sounded like its opposite. "Yeah . . . only he didn't have some sea witch trying to kill him."

"I thought we were forgetting that."

"Now we're remembering it." She touched Will's knee, and he looked at her. "What am I supposed to do?"

Will's eyes widened slightly, and he shook his head.

"Mist, vapor, wind. How do you get rid of something like that?"

"I don't know." Will thought for a moment. "But it seems like . . . it seems like, if she wants to be in this world, she has to have some kind of corporeal form. She has to be clinging to something—human body, water molecules."

Gretchen remembered something. "Kirk was trying to kill himself to get rid of her. Would that have worked?"

"Maybe if you can destroy the body while she's in it, you destroy her."

"I'd settle for sending her back to the spirit world," Gretchen said.

"We don't know how to do that, either," Will pointed out.

The sound of the leaf blower died away suddenly, making their silence seem thicker. Gretchen watched as an ant crawled across the spine of an overturned leaf. She wondered about that ant. Did it have a soul? Some sort of ant essence that surpassed its bodily form? Or if she leaned over and crushed it between two fingers, would that ant cease to exist forever, snuffed out like a candle?

"So . . . if she was mist . . ." Gretchen bit her lip, trying to remember what she had learned so far in AP chemistry. "I suppose you could separate water molecules."

"Wouldn't that take a nuclear explosion?" Will asked. "Or something like that?"

"You don't like my plan?" Gretchen asked dryly.

"Not if it involves bombing Walfang." Will picked up a twig and poked at the mossy earth. "Maybe— instead of getting rid of her—maybe we could try to catch her."

"Like how?"

"I don't know. If she's mist, maybe we could freeze her."

"Like with liquid nitrogen or something?"

"Yeah."

"Then we'd have a Circe popsicle," Gretchen joked. "We could keep her in the freezer."

"We have a big one in the basement," Will offered. "Put her in next to the peas."

"The sad thing is, this is our best idea."

"I don't know where we'd get liquid nitrogen, any- way," Will admitted. "Stuff like that only shows up when you're in a *Terminator* movie."

"I don't even know how we could contain her in the first place," Gretchen said. "How would we pour liquid nitrogen on her?"

"No clue."

Gretchen sighed. Will gave her a sad, uneven smile. She scooted over and rested her head in his lap. Will picked up a long length of her blond hair and plucked a leaf out of it. Then he stroked her hair, combing it out with his fingers.

Gretchen closed her eyes. It was cool under the tree, but not cold. She could feel the warmth from Will's leg pressed against her cheek.

I wish I could stay here, she thought. *Right here, in this moment.*

But she knew, even as she had the thought, that the moment was already passing away. Dying, like the falling yellow leaves above her, which floated gently to the earth to disappear into the soil forever.

Gretchen checked the number in the text on her mobile phone. Thirty-three. She stared at the door. There was a metal three screwed into the wood. Beside it was a faded pale wood three, a shadow left by the second metal number when it fell off long ago. The hallway smelled stale, of old smoke and disinfectant. The walls were a depressing shade of mauve—the kind abandoned in the early eighties—and were marked here and there with unexplained dark smudges, per- haps left by furniture moved in and out, evidence of the transient nature of the building.

With a sigh, she knocked. Kirk hadn't been in school, so she'd left at lunch. Frankly, she needed to talk to him more than she needed calculus. There was no sound behind the door, so she counted to ten and knocked again. Finally a slow shuffling step ap- proached the door. For a moment Gretchen worried that Angus had sent her the wrong address—that this was the home of an elderly or disabled person—but after a brief pause, the door opened a crack and a large dark eye peeked out.

"What do you want?" Kirk asked. He didn't sound defensive, just curious. Still, he didn't open the door any wider, not even a small fraction.

"I want to talk to you."

"What about?"

Gretchen hesitated before answering. Finally she decided that there was no way to hedge the truth. "There's a sea witch who's trying to kill me."

Kirk drew in a deep breath, then blew it out. "Okay," he said, opening the door. "I guess you'd better come in." Gretchen winced at the sight of his face—he had an enormous black eye and bruises on his forehead.

Gretchen stepped through the doorway and shut the door behind her. Kirk wore an oversized gray sweatshirt and baggy jeans, and as she followed him down the hall into the living room, she noticed that his feet had on only thick white cotton socks. The room was lined with windows on two walls and wouldn't have been so ugly if it hadn't been for the brown carpet that covered the floor and the lumpy gray couch that looked as if someone had rescued it from the side of the road after a heavy rain. A distressingly nicked-up coffee table was covered in books and fashion magazines. The walls were completely bare.

"No television," Gretchen remarked.

"It bothers me," Kirk said, rubbing his forehead. "So my sister keeps it in her bedroom."

"Is it just the two of you here?"

"That's enough, believe me." Kirk flopped onto the couch and pulled a faded gray *Star Wars* comforter over his legs.

"Where's your mother?"

Kirk looked out the window at the bare tree in the yard. "Who knows?"

Gretchen pursed her lips. A pass-through kitchen looked out on the dreary living room. Dirty bowls and cups overflowed from the sink to the counter. "Is Adelaide at work?"

"Yeah." Kirk followed Gretchen's gaze. "I should probably clean that up before she gets home." His large eyes met Gretchen's. "I've been saying that for three days."

Gretchen nodded. "I know how that goes." There was no place for Gretchen to sit, so she simply plopped onto the floor and tucked her legs beneath her. Her long white woolen scarf rested on the brown carpet on either side of her knees, like fallen snow.

"So—you're being haunted by a witch," Kirk prompted, as if that were a perfectly normal way to open a conversation.

"Right. You're familiar with the witch."

"Oh, is that what that was?" Kirk pointed to his face.

"According to Asia."

"Asia. The Siren."

"She's come to help us," Gretchen explained.

"Has she?" The words were brittle and dry as old paper.

"Yes." But now Gretchen wasn't so sure. *She was going to hand me over to Calypso before.*

Kirk's right eyebrow went up over his bruised eye, and Gretchen wondered if it hurt him to do it. "Do you trust her?" he asked.

Will trusts her, Gretchen thought. "I think so."

"Why?"

Gretchen was at a loss. "I don't know," she admitted.

Kirk lay back on the sofa and looked up at the white ceiling, which was textured in looping swirls. "Gretchen, I know everyone thinks I'm crazy."

"I don't think you're crazy." Gretchen said the words, then wondered if they were true. She did think that Kirk was crazy. Sometimes. But not always. At important times he was completely sane. He was just . . . sensitive. As if he could hear things broadcast on a radio frequency that couldn't be picked up by other people.

Kirk looked at her sideways, then back up at the ceiling. "It's okay if you do. I just hope you'll listen to me."

"I'm listening. That's why I'm here."

"I think you should find out what Asia wants. Then you need to ask yourself if that's what you want."

Gretchen found herself staring up at the ceiling, too. She stretched out on the brown carpet and lay on her back. She imagined she was lying on the ground, staring up at the stars. "What I want doesn't seem to have anything to do with anything," she admitted.

"Maybe it isn't fair, but I don't trust her."

"She's different from the others," Gretchen said.

"All we know is what she tells us, right?"

This statement fell like snow—soft and cold—over Gretchen. "She says that Circe wants to possess me. To take my power."

Kirk didn't ask what power. He didn't ask any-thing. Finally Gretchen went on: "She thinks I have to destroy Circe before Circe destroys me."

Kirk didn't reply. A phone rang in the apartment next door. Someone answered it, and Gretchen heard the low tones of someone talking.

Kirk rolled over to look at Gretchen. She craned her neck to catch his eye.

"Why don't you ask Mafer?" Kirk suggested. "About Asia?"

"Mafer?" Gretchen repeated.

Kirk pinkened. "You're friends, right? I've seen you together."

"Yeah, but—"

"Mafer knows things about people sometimes," Kirk said. He pulled the *Star Wars* comforter up to his chin. He looked like a young boy, and Gretchen wished that she were his older sister instead of Adelaide. He deserved to have someone who understood him, some-one who could take care of him.

"I'll ask her, Kirk," Gretchen said.

"Good."

Gretchen's feet ached. It was the end of her shift, and she'd been pulling double duty as waitress and bus-boy, since Kirk was still recovering. Will was perched on a stool at the counter, waiting, as Gretchen pulled off her apron.

"You headin' home, hon?" Lisette put a tentative hand on her shoulder.

"Yeah."

"If you see Kirk, you tell him we're . . . thinking of him, okay?" She looked up at Gretchen with damp, dark eyes ringed in heavy black shadow.

Angel scowled from behind the cook's window.

Gretchen lifted her eyebrows at Lisette, who bit her lip. She stuck a pencil into her bright orange bun and turned away.

Gretchen looked over at Will, expecting him to be frowning over the mention of Kirk's name. Instead, he just gave her a compassionate smile that—finally— seemed to grasp that Kirk's problems were not his own fault. In many ways, Gretchen and Kirk were alike. They couldn't help what they were.

Will followed Gretchen to the door and reached for it, holding it open as she passed through. It was an unexpected, gentlemanly gesture, and it made Gretchen smile. She stepped out onto the brick land- ing and inhaled the misty air that held just an edge of autumn cool. The light of a street lamp caught a col- umn of cloud in its beam. Gretchen felt the drops on her eyelashes as she hesitated at the foot of the steps.

"Should we get going?" Will asked, but Gretchen shook her head.

"I'm waiting for someone."

As if on cue, someone shouted, "Gretchen?" A mo- ment later, Mafer materialized through the dense fog. She looked up at Will with a strange hesitation in her face. Gretchen noticed it but couldn't interpret its meaning.

"What's up?" Will asked, his eyes flashing from Mafer to Gretchen.

"Mafer's coming over to hang out," Gretchen announced. "I'll drop her off at home later."

Mafer nodded, and Will shrugged. He stood on the pavement with his hands in his pockets, watching Gretchen as she walked to the driver's side. She placed her key in the door lock, but a moment before she turned it, her eye caught a subtle movement. A downstroke, almost like a finger tracing a letter, appeared on the driver's side window, parting the droplets of mist that had gathered there. Then a curve. Another curve.

Gretchen stared. It was the letter *B*. She took a step backward in surprise.

Then an almost triangle—an *A*. A curve. *C*. The sharp, twiglike *K*. *BACK*.

Mafer screamed, and Gretchen barely had time to process the letters before she heard the squeal of tires up the street.

"Get back!" Will shouted.

She was caught in the headlights for a moment, but she dove backward into the street as the car raced forward and slammed full speed into the Gremlin. There was a rattle as a hubcap fell off and rolled away. Silence. Then the car backed up with a horrible screech, and Gretchen raced forward.

She didn't think—she was pure action as she leaped onto the hood of the car, pressing her face against the windshield. She slammed her fist through the thick glass and felt a flash of surprise when it yielded, bending and shattering. The car sped forward and, all at once, the interior was lit with brilliant light that illuminated the face of the driver—a young woman whose expression was contorted and whose golden eyes glittered with cold rage. She screamed as the light blinded her, and threw her arm over her eyes. The car swerved, and Gretchen was thrown onto the asphalt as it sped into a street lamp and was still.

Angel ran out of the diner. "What the hell is going on?" he cried when he saw the car. "Holy shit!" He ran back inside, shouting to Lisette to call the police.

The street was silent as death for a moment, and then—once again—the car leaped to life. It backed away from the street lamp and screeched down the street.

Gretchen watched the fading red taillights disappear around the corner. She had fallen over the edge of the curb on the other side of the street, sprawling over the sidewalk. When she looked down, she saw that her jeans were ripped at the knee.

"Gretchen!" Will ran to her side.

She looked up at his face. He was staring after the car, as if daring it to come back. But it wouldn't return, Gretchen knew that.

Will helped her stand, wobbly on liquid knees. She clung to his elbow as they walked over to the Gremlin. The side was smashed, and the force of the car had driven the front of the Gremlin into the rear of the car parked before it. She stared at the place where she would have been crushed against the twisted metal.

She felt Mafer looking at her. "What just happened?"

"I don't know."

"You lit that car with lightning," Mafer pressed.

"I didn't mean to," Gretchen said, but even as the

words passed her lips, she doubted them. She *had* meant to. She had wanted to see the driver. There was even a part of her that would have killed the driver if she'd had the chance. The thought made her tremble. *Was that what I wanted?* Gretchen wondered. *Or is it what Tisiphone wanted? What's the difference between being Tisiphone and being possessed by Circe?*

Shaking, she looked over at her car. The glass on the driver's side had shattered, erasing the letters that had appeared there, and Gretchen wondered if she had ever really seen them at all. That was when she noticed that Will was staring at the same place.

"Back," Gretchen said.

Will gaped at her. "You saw that?"

Mafer gasped, and they both looked at her.

Gretchen felt as if she were falling—she could almost hear the wind rushing past her ears. "You too?"

Mafer's brown eyes were wide. "Yes."

"It was a warning. You both saw it. Something tried to kill me, and something tried to warn me."

Mafer nodded.

Gretchen didn't need to waste time wondering what was trying to kill her. That much was obvious. But the other was still a mystery. "Was it . . . the ghost?" Gretchen asked.

"It's . . ." Mafer looked at Will. Even in the dim, cloudy light of the street lamp, Gretchen could see her hesitation. She gazed at Will, who seemed sick and pale. The moisture glistened on him like a fever. It was clear that Mafer wouldn't speak—not unless Will wanted her to.

Gretchen turned to him. "What is it?"

"I don't know." Will's voice was a whisper.

"Don't you?" Mafer's gaze was piercing, and Will winced beneath it, as if he were in physical pain.

"Do *you*?" Gretchen demanded, turning to Mafer.

But still, Mafer was watching Will.

"Stop looking at him," Gretchen snapped. She was glad that Kirk had told her to talk to Mafer, because it was clear that Mafer knew. She knew something that Will didn't want her to know, and it made Gretchen furious.

Finally Mafer seemed to reach a decision. "Gretchen—"

"Stop," Will said, putting up a hand, but Mafer ignored him.

"The spirit that's trying to protect you . . ."

Suddenly Gretchen knew, as if Mafer's mind had communicated it without words, and a new kind of dread filled her. "Don't say it," she whispered. She looked over at Will. His hands covered his face, and his body was bent, like a branch in a cruel wind.

"Gretchen, it's Will's brother."

"No."

"It's Tim."

Chapter Twenty

From the Walfang Gazette
Police Led on High-Speed Chase

Walfang police were led on a high-speed chase down a section of Route 27 last night as an unknown driver hit speeds of up to ninety miles per hour. The car was a 2007 Nissan, reported stolen by Samantha Munch earlier in the evening. After leading police on a chase for more than fifteen miles, the car jumped the median and flew out of control, finally coming to a stop as it hit a tree. Police exited their vehicle and approached the car, but the driver must have fled the scene. "I don't know how he got by us," said Officer Bradley Vincent. "But it was pitch dark outside."

Detectives are working on a partial thumbprint left at the scene. . . .

He pulled the flute from his bottom drawer, testing its weight in his fingers. It was light, like a breath of air. Will tucked the ancient instrument into the inside pocket of his jacket, then closed his bureau and started out the door.

Johnny was in the kitchen when Will reached downstairs. Johnny's pale skin was drawn over the bones of his face. He looked taut, like one of his guitar strings tuned sharp. He hadn't taken the news of

Gretchen's latest accident well, and looking at the dark circles beneath his eyes, Will wondered whether he had slept at all. Johnny didn't speak, just gave Will a half smile that was more reflex than greeting, and took a long pull of his coffee.

"Didn't sleep?" Will asked.

Johnny shook his head. "It's hard—being in Tim's room." He shifted in his chair, and the wood creaked beneath him.

Will didn't reply. Instead, he reached for one of the blueberry scones that his mother had left out on a plate and took a bite.

"You can see the ocean from up there," Johnny went on. "Sometimes I even think I can hear it." He looked up at Will. "It's strange, how time passes. The waves roll on, the minutes come one after the other. The days pile up, and you don't even notice. And then one day it can all be over." He wrapped his hands around the coffee mug.

"Gretchen's okay," Will said.

Johnny looked at him, doubt written in his dark eyes. "I know you want to protect her, Will. So do I. But . . ." He stared down into his coffee. "You can't protect anyone."

"You're wrong." Johnny looked up at the edge in Will's voice, but Will didn't care. He was shaking, almost burning with rage. This was the attitude that he despised most. "And even if you aren't wrong," Will went on, "I'm not about to stop trying." He started for the door.

"Will—" Johnny called, but Will didn't turn back.

Reaching into his jacket, he kept a tight hold on the flute, half afraid that it might fall out of his jacket and be lost forever.

He hurried down the path that he and Gretchen had worn to the bay. A light drizzle was falling, casting the clouds and water in shades of dark blue and pale gray. Will reached the top of the escarpment and blew into the instrument. Then he sat down on the wet grass to wait.

The clouds were a thick mass, impenetrable and blank as a wall. They formed no shapes, nor did the water. Because of the rain and chill air, there were no people. All was still. There was nothing to watch to make the time go faster. He was alone with his thoughts, which were jumbled together like the stuff in his mother's junk drawer. The moment he landed on something, such as Tim, or Gretchen saving him, his mind's eye caught sight of something else—Kirk, or the fire on the bay. It was distracting and nonsensical, worse than useless. But there was too much junk to close the drawer. All he could do was sit and stare helplessly at all the stuff.

He didn't have to wait long before Asia appeared. Will hurried down the embankment to meet her. She was walking on the shore, wearing an olive trench coat over blue jeans. Her dark hair was loose around her face, her lips and cheeks red with the weather.

"Where have you been?" Will asked.

"Nearby," Asia said. "I expected you'd call to me."

Will looked out over the water. "It's so strange to

see you again. I keep thinking that . . . now anything
could happen. Tim could walk out of that water."

"I'm not back from the dead, Will. I was never
dead."

Will turned to face her. "In my mind, you were dead."

Asia reached for his hand. "I'm sorry for the pain I
caused you." She intertwined her fingers with his.

Warmth flowed from her hand into his, traveling
up his arm and down the side of his body, like a
caress.

"I did not think I would return," Asia admitted. "I
thought it was better if you and Gretchen assumed
I was dead."

"Why did you come back?" Will asked.

Asia dropped his hand. "I had to, Will. When I realized that Circe was here, I had to."

"How did you even know she was?"

Asia looked down, traced an arc in the sand with
her toe. "Tim told me," she admitted finally.

Will felt this answer like a slap. "My brother?"

"The Beyond has a new kind of vibrancy—a new
access to our plane," Asia explained.

"Is that, like, the dead? Heaven?"

"I don't know what heaven is, Will. I can only tell
you that it's a different plane. And there are planes
beyond that. I've never been there. I've never seen it.
But I can feel it."

"How did you see Tim, then?"

"The spirits have new access to our world. Access
they don't usually have. Tim came to me in a dream."

"But that was just a dream."

"Who is to say what a dream is? We have access to all sorts of things in our dreams, Will. Things that slip away on waking."

Will remembered the dreams he'd had lately: A dream of a dragon lighting a lake of oil. A dream that he was with his brother, sitting on a dock. A dream about Gretchen, setting the bay on fire. And the letters in the mirror: *FURY.* And on the car . . .

"You've remembered something," Asia said.

"Just . . . dreams." Will shifted his weight. Just dreams. Just. Or had Tim been sending him messages? His throat tightened at the thought that his brother had been trying to tell him things and he'd missed them, or feared them, not recognizing them for what they were. Mafer knew, but he didn't—not until the last time.

Asia nodded knowingly. "You see now."

Will rubbed the scar that ran along his forehead. "I don't know." He focused on taking one breath followed by another. "How do we destroy Circe?"

"I don't know."

"You're lying."

"I don't lie."

"You aren't telling the whole truth, then."

Asia sighed. "I don't know how you can destroy her. All I can tell you is that you may be able to banish her back to the Beyond by destroying the body she inhabits."

"Like Kirk was trying to do."

"Yes."

"So we have to find someone who's willing to kill himself."

Asia didn't respond.

"Boy, Asia, you're just full of good news, aren't you?" Will's voice was bitter. "You've always got some little nugget of wonderful to pass around."

"I did not bring these things into being, Will. They are the way they are. I can't change them."

Will tried to speak, but he was blinded and strangled by tears. "Somebody else has to die now," he choked out.

"I don't know." Asia grasped his hand again. "Perhaps there is another way. I just don't know, Will."

"Can Tim help protect Gretchen?"

"He already has, I think," Asia said. "He can see her when we cannot. But I don't know what more he can do. He doesn't exist in this world."

"God*damn* it." Will choked on a sob, and Asia pressed his fingers.

"I wish I had some comfort for you," she said.

Will rubbed his palms over his cheeks, brushing away his tears. Some comfort. Something to cling to. Instead, there was only certain pain, certain death. Because Will knew one thing—there was no way that he was going to let that thing get anywhere near Gretchen. He would die first. He would die and send that thing back to hell, where it belonged. So there was no comfort there. But at least he didn't have to face the thing alone. Will took a deep breath, feeling, at last, some small comfort and gratitude. "You're here," Will said at last.

"Yes," Asia said. "And she was sent to the Beyond once."

"How?"

"I know only that Calypso used Circe's own magic against her. But I don't know how."

Will sat down, and Asia sat beside him. They both looked out where the air was still and gray over the dark water. His brother was out there, somewhere. He saw now what it was that Tim had wanted from him all along. He'd wanted Gretchen to know about her powers, perhaps so that she could use them. But Will hadn't told her. In trying to protect her, he might have caused more harm than good.

"What will we do the next time?" Will asked. "Could she—could Gretchen go somewhere? Hide?"

Asia touched the rocky sand beneath them with long, pale fingers. "I can only tell you that fear is the enemy," she said. "Running won't help. There is only one way for this to end—Gretchen must face Circe. And I do not know how that will end."

Will watched her profile, suddenly wary. Asia's black hair streamed down her back; her brilliant green eyes were facing out to sea. He remembered with an almost physical reaction that at one time she had been sent to kill Gretchen. She was supposed to deliver Gretchen to Calypso. What if this were the same thing? What if she regretted her decision not to kill Gretchen the last time?

Asia looked at him then, her cool green eyes piercing him like an arrow. He wanted to trust her, but he feared her as well. A moment ago, he had been grateful for her help. Now he felt wary of accepting it.

I can't trust anyone to help Gretchen, he realized. *Everyone else has their own agenda.* Will didn't know if he could protect Gretchen, but he was sure that he would never let anything hurt her. *I'll die protecting her,* he vowed, and the thought of death didn't frighten him in the least. In that way, Asia had been right. Once you gave up fear, you regained your power.

Chapter Twenty-One

Gretchen realized that her wrists were no longer bound. She lifted her arms and looked down to see them lined with flaming feathers.

Still she burned on.

Sparks flew from her body, swept like a wave over the scarecrow man. His dark clothes ignited, and she saw his form, black and wrapped in fire as he fell to the ground. Someone threw a cloak over him, but when the flames died away, he did not move.

The humming through Gretchen's body reached a fevered pitch, and then stopped, seeming to extinguish the light. The fire had gone out. The people had disappeared.

Above her, there were no stars.

She was nowhere.

Someone was seated on the front step of the Archer house, arms folded on knees, head bowed. For a crazy moment, Gretchen thought the figure was Tim. The way the figure sat reminded her of the last night that she had seen him. He had been sitting on a rock, down by the bay, in this same posture. She wanted to roll down the window, call out to him. But the figure moved slightly, and a long lock of brown hair fell forward, over the right shoulder.

Sadness welled up in Gretchen then, like the pressure from a geyser rising to the surface. She felt it might explode out of her, coating everyone in hot steam. But in another moment the car had slowed and things had shifted just enough that the pressure eased, and the next moment it passed away.

That was the thing about this world. Nothing stayed forever—even things that seemed permanent, like rocks, or love. Eventually the sea would swallow them up, or the earth would shift, or things would change in some other way, and the thing you loved would be gone, or different, and so would your love for it. Even the memory would alter or fade, until you didn't even have that to cling to.

These were dark, bitter thoughts, and Gretchen forced her mind to move away from them. *I can't think this way. All I can do is think about the now. This moment. This is what really exists.*

She stopped the car and turned back to the figure on the steps. Even though Gretchen couldn't see her face, she could tell by the thick brown hair that it was Mafer. Relief flooded her system. They hadn't had a chance to talk the night before, and Gretchen desperately needed to. *Of course Mafer knew that.*

Gretchen wondered what it would be like to know things about people, to be able to guess things in advance. She'd had that experience once or twice—knowing who was calling the moment the phone rang, predicting the next song on the radio—but had always been able to write it off as coincidence. She wondered if Mafer ever felt burdened by what she knew about people. Whether she, like Gretchen, might rather have a normal life, free of the "gift."

Mafer didn't look up as Gretchen pulled her father's car into the driveway, or even when Gretchen crunched across the gravel and up the stone footpath that led to the porch. When Gretchen reached her step, Mafer finally lifted her chin and placed it on her crossed arms. Her dark eyes caught a ray of sunlight, which made them seem almost hazel.

"Are you okay?" Gretchen asked.

"Define okay," Mafer replied.

Gretchen huffed out a sigh. "Do you want to come inside?"

Mafer nodded. "Yeah."

Gretchen led Mafer through the front door, past the formal living room, and into the kitchen. "Can I get you some water?" Gretchen asked, tossing her jacket over the back of a chair.

"Nothing, thanks." Mafer leaned against a counter as Gretchen pulled a glass from the cupboard. She filled it from the tap and took a long pull. The Archers got their water from a well, and it had a sour, metallic aftertaste, but Gretchen was used to it. She wrapped her hands around the glass and turned to face her friend.

"Thank God you're here."

Mafer closed her eyes. "You don't seem surprised to see me."

"I'm relieved," Gretchen admitted. "I was going to come over to your house today anyway."

"Were you?" Mafer's eyes fluttered open, and she

cocked her head, a small smile at the edge of her lips. "Really?"

"I wanted to talk to you about something." Gretchen ran her fingers through her long hair, impatiently tucking it behind an ear. "We didn't get a chance last night. I have a question."

"All right."

"There's someone I'm wondering . . ." Gretchen's throat felt dry; she took another sip of water. "I'm wondering if I can trust this person."

There was a window over the sink, and Mafer looked out to where the brown fields led out to the bay beyond. Gretchen could see two figures in the distance. They were walking toward the house. There was a glare on the window, and Gretchen couldn't see the figures properly, but she assumed it was the Archers, or maybe her father and Mrs. Archer, out for a walk. "Someone who has returned after a long absence," Mafer said in a dreamy voice.

"Yes." Relief flooded Gretchen's body at the fact that she didn't have to explain all about Asia. *Of course not; Mafer already knows.* "How can I know whether or not I can trust her?"

Mafer turned to face her. "What makes you think you can?"

Gretchen was about to say that she was Asia's friend, but the words wouldn't quite force themselves out. *Can you ever be friends with someone who was originally sent to kill you? True, in the end, she changed her mind . . . but that didn't change what Asia was sent to do.* "I don't know." An image of Asia popped into Gretchen's mind—Asia ready to kill Kirk when she thought Circe was inhabiting his body. At the time, Gretchen had taken this to mean that Asia was willing to protect her at all costs. But now a new thought occurred to her. *Life does not mean much to Asia,* Gretchen realized. *She's ready to kill if she has to.*

"Is there some reason for you *not* to trust her?" Mafer asked, and as the words floated into the air, Gretchen felt herself again looking out the window. "Is there anything she might want?"

Now the glare had shifted, and the two figures came into view in the purple twilight of the fast-fading sun. One was Will, the other Asia. The breeze lifted Asia's long hair slightly, blowing it away from her face, revealing her brilliant green eyes. She looked impossibly graceful and beautiful, even in the old clothes she wore. With a sinking feeling in her stomach Gretchen whispered, "Maybe there is something she wants."

That's why she's here, she knew in a flash. *This has nothing to do with Circe. It has to do with me. With Will. She wants to get rid of me.*

Maybe she is *Circe.*

Gretchen frowned. She looked down at her right hand and snapped her fingers. A flame shot up between them, and burned there—steady. She played with it, letting it roll over the backs of her fingers, then out to the tips.

Opening her palm, she let the flame settle inside, then quickly closed her hand. The flame snuffed out.

"You've learned something," Mafer noted.

Gretchen turned to face her. She had forgotten that her friend was in the room.

But Mafer didn't look surprised. "That's good."

"I'm not sure how I did it."

"You'll figure it out."

Gretchen turned away, and Mafer placed a gentle hand on her back. "Gretchen, this thing . . . it's never going to leave you alone. It's seeking you. I could feel its hatred." Gretchen looked into her friend's face and read the terror in her eyes. "It's not going to stop."

"Then I'll have to stop it," Gretchen said simply.

"Do you think you can?"

"No," Gretchen admitted. "But I have to try."

The sun had gone down by the time Will and Asia neared the farmhouse. Gretchen was waiting for them on the steps. She had left Mafer inside. She wanted to face Asia alone.

Will dropped Asia's hand as Gretchen approached them. The sun had dipped below the horizon, and the sky was darkening fast.

Gretchen said nothing as she walked up to Asia. She looked into those green eyes, luminous as sea glass. Asia looked back at her, unflinching, and Gretchen felt the familiar drop in temperature that came whenever she was close to the Siren.

"Leave us, Will," Asia said.

"What? No."

Gretchen turned to him. "Please, Will." But he just shook his head. She sighed. *I should have expected that,* she thought. She knew it was hopeless—there was no way she would get him to leave them alone. But she guessed it didn't really matter. What she had to say to Asia could be said in front of Will. "Why are you here, Asia?" Gretchen demanded.

"To help you."

"Really?" Gretchen looked at Will, who was frowning at her. He shook his head slightly, almost in warning. But Gretchen ignored him. "Why should I trust you?"

Asia smiled a little then. "You don't?"

"No."

"That's wise."

Gretchen felt her heart clench. The darkness around them deepened and grew. "Are you saying that I shouldn't trust you?"

"I'm saying that you shouldn't trust anyone, Gretchen."

"Gretchen—" Will began, but an unreadable look came over Asia's face. Gretchen steeled herself just in time—with movements like lightning, Asia leaped toward Gretchen, unleashing a primeval shriek.

Gretchen clawed at Asia, and a flame shot from her fingers. But Asia's reach missed Gretchen. Instead, the Siren crashed against a human form that had just come through the door, knocking her from the steps to the ground.

Gretchen's ears rang with Asia's scream of agony, and a moment later, pain coursed through her own arm. A gleam of silver flashed in the near-darkness. It took several seconds for her mind to process what was happening. Mafer and Asia struggled on the ground. Mafer was holding a knife; her eyes glowed gold.

Gretchen had started toward them when the truth turned her cold. Asia hadn't been possessed by Circe— Mafer had.

Will shouted as Asia wrestled the knife from Mafer's hand. It clattered away, and Will ran to pick it up. Asia slammed her arm across Mafer's throat, choking the life out of her.

"Stop!" Gretchen screamed. "Asia, stop!"

But Asia didn't hear, or maybe she wasn't listening. She landed a knee on Mafer's chest, then another, and Gretchen watched as Mafer's face began to turn blue. Her friend would be dead in moments if she didn't do something.

Lightning tore across the sky in a jagged streak as Gretchen leaped onto Asia. The Siren shook her off, but Gretchen leaped again. Lightning exploded nearby, illuminating the cloudless sky for a fraction of a second. Gretchen tore at Asia until the Siren's arm came away from Mafer's throat.

Mafer took a heaving gasp, then opened her mouth wide. A steady stream of dark mist, thick and oily as rank smoke, poured from between her lips. It hung there for a moment. Something slammed into Gretchen. She twisted and writhed, trying to get a hold on the thing, but it slipped through her fingers like shadow.

It has its own form now, Gretchen realized. In the moonlight, she saw something like fierce teeth, and the creature lunged at her, piercing her shoulder.

Gretchen screamed in pain.

"I can't see it!" Will shouted as the cloud shadow dragged Gretchen across the yard. Asia raced forward, but the creature flung her backward.

Gretchen fought, but the vapor was powerful, and she felt its desire—the desire to drown Gretchen, to snuff her out like a candle flame and rule in her body.

Desperate, Gretchen tore at the ground, clinging to the rocky surface. But with a powerful heave, the vapor slammed her against a tree. Beside her was the water trough the goats drank from.

Pain shot through Gretchen as she struggled to her feet. The cloud-shadow landed noiselessly beside her. Gretchen ran to the left, but the creature pounced, pinning her to the earth.

Gretchen felt the fire burning through her, like acid in her veins, and a brilliant light poured from her hands. But the cloud expanded and filled, quenching the light, gobbling it up. It reared back, lifting its hideous jaws.

It plunged forward, and Gretchen felt piercing cold as the thing tore through her.

And at the same time, Gretchen felt a thickening fog enter her mind.

She saw Asia leaping toward her, Will behind her, running, too. But Gretchen saw them as if she were looking through the wrong end of a telescope—they seemed small and far away. Gretchen's ears were full of wax. She couldn't hear properly—only muffled noises. Her body was leaden, as if it had been dipped in bronze. She knew she was moving, but she had no control over her limbs.

It was Circe who controlled her now.

Asia pinned Gretchen's arms to her sides, but she felt nothing as Asia dragged her toward the water trough. *She'll drown me,* Gretchen realized. *She'll kill the both of us—Circe and me.*

But then Will was there. He tore at Asia, trying to pull Gretchen from her grasp, but the Siren wouldn't be stopped. Asia landed a fierce blow against his chest, sending him sprawling, but Gretchen felt no emotion as Asia pulled at her hair, yanking it back, and made ready to plunge her face-first into the trough.

But Circe wasn't about to let that happen. Gretchen's body struggled away from Asia's grip, then flung the Siren away, sending her across the grass like a skipping stone.

Gretchen could feel Circe's elation, the thrill she felt at conquest. Gretchen was powerless. Powerless, and growing weaker. With every second, she felt her sense of self disappearing.

Will staggered to his feet as Gretchen's field of vision narrowed, turning to a tiny pinpoint.

The moment was passing.

Summoning all of her strength, Gretchen flexed her mind, and in an instant, she felt herself burning with a light bright enough to cut through the darkness of the universe, like a star. Lightning lit up the Archer fields as Gretchen burned with enough heat to melt cities, enough light to turn night into day. She felt her flesh falling from her. Gretchen felt the pain, but did not feel it. She knew it, but did not mind it. She would die now, this she knew.

She would die, and so would Circe.

She remembered all of this as her body flared into flame. She was burning, she knew it, and the shadow inside her reveled in the new power. But Gretchen burned on, burned brighter. And the silver stars above grew larger and seemed to come nearer, and Gretchen felt herself turn white-hot, lighting the field until the ground beneath her was the color of bone.

Circe shrieked then, and seemed to shrink, and the stars seemed to reach for Gretchen's fire, streaking toward her like silver rain, like the night of the meteor shower.

Gretchen burned on, and she screamed in pain, but she was not consumed. She turned her face to the sky, releasing her voice upward, and suddenly a silver cloud appeared out of the rain of stars. Circe howled at the cloud, but it grew, and Gretchen thought she could see faces in it—Tim's face, and the faces of others. Dimly, she realized that these were the dead. Tim was leading them, pulling them forward, through the rift between worlds and toward Circe. Circe screamed as they reached down and tore at Gretchen.

They tore at her body, but she did not feel it. They tore at her and through her, reaching inside, to the shade that inhabited her. Circe resisted—the cloud-shadow clung and sucked at Gretchen, but the arms held strong, and soon they pulled Circe up, up into their cloud. Their silver brilliance erased the shadow, or swallowed it, and then the wind pulled and howled with so much force that Gretchen felt as if her soul were being yanked from her body. The air only served to fan the flames.

From a distance, she heard Will's voice shouting something; a word she knew but could not place. Gretchen burned on and on, and only slowly felt the light around her fade, and the stars return to their normal size and recede back into the heavens. She felt herself disappearing. The sky above was dark again, and the field was lit with faraway fires. Gretchen closed her eyes, one arm on the cool grass.

Someone whispered her name, and she imagined that she saw Will bending over her, weeping. Behind him stood Asia. *I would have died for you,* Gretchen heard Will say, but she could hardly make sense of the words. *I never would have let him die. Never.*

And still, she felt herself diminishing, like a spark into the night sky.

I am dying, she thought, and there was enough of her left to feel reassurance and even a trace of happiness as her vision closed and everything went black.

Epilogue

"Come on, Will!" Angus shouted, waving to him from the ice. His barn jacket was open, revealing a plaid shirt, and he wore a cap pulled low on his head, his curls sticking out madly. His long wild limbs only made it more comical when he glided gracefully across the ice. "Come show us your *Disney on Ice* moves," he urged, spinning into a lazy turn.

"Nobody can compete with Goofy," Will replied.

Mafer let out a shriek as Angus glided into her, and they both spilled onto the ice, laughing.

Gretchen squinted at the blue sky. Cotton-ball clouds drifted across the expanse, seeming unhurried and untroubled. She was resting on a bench beside the lake. Will shifted beside her, as if the cold air was starting to chill him. He put an arm around Gretchen and pulled her closer.

She wore only a light corduroy jacket and no hat. Her long hair spilled down her back, white as the fresh snow that blanketed the ground, white as the clouds above. She was smiling, watching Will and Mafer goof around, but she had no urge to join them. She was happy here, on the bench.

Taking off his jacket, Will started to put it around her shoulders, but she shrugged it off. She turned to him, still smiling. "I don't need it."

Will slipped an arm back into his sleeve and shrugged on his jacket. "You still don't get cold."

Gretchen shook her head.

He touched her cheek with a gloved hand. She put her own bare palm over his and closed her eyes. She liked to imagine that she was warming him.

There had been no fires, not for weeks. Her room was finished, and she and her father had moved back into their own house, which was finally starting to feel familiar and comfortable. The boxes in the living room were unpacked, and with the addition of new things and objects and books from the Manhattan apartment, her room looked like a place where she belonged. It looked like home.

Even school had settled down. It had been hard, but Gretchen had almost completely caught up with all of the work she had let slide the first few weeks. Now she had to concentrate on pulling her college applications together—but there was still time. She was considering taking a gap year, anyway. She still had a lot to sort out.

The kids in the hall had stopped giving her sideways looks, and even the gossip about Kirk was disappearing, now that he'd managed to act normal for a few months. And yes, she was still warm, as if she carried her own fire inside. But she was no longer hot. No longer ready to flame out of control. She had no idea what it meant. Will liked to believe that she had burned through her power, that she was a mere mortal now. Gretchen liked to believe that, too, when she could manage it.

But mostly she just didn't know what to believe. Circe, Asia—all of that seemed like a dream, one she could barely recall, could only get a vague sense of. Mostly, it left her with a feeling of relief that it was over.

But sometimes she caught sight of herself in the mirror and felt a shock at her own stark hair. It had turned white the night Circe found her.

The events of that night had unfolded clearly for her only afterward, with Asia's help. Circe had seen her moment—her power was great enough to inhabit a shadow form and attack. Gretchen had burned, burned to ash, burned to death. But she didn't die— she couldn't really die, not yet. It wasn't her time. And in burning and dying and yet not dying, she had ripped wide open the slit in the fabric between the living and the dead. Tim had been there, and an army of the dead—all of the men and women who had fallen to Circe's power. Their power had flared under Gretchen's fire, and they had reached down and pulled Circe back into the Beyond.

Still, whenever Gretchen recalled that night, she felt a sense of vertigo as she tried to piece together what it all meant.

Am I Tisiphone?

Am I Gretchen?

She could get lost in the what-ifs. *What if I live five*

hundred years? What if the power hasn't left? What if Circe returns?

She wanted reassurance, a written guarantee that things were going to work out fine. *But no one gets that.*

Gretchen looked up at the sky again, imagining the Beyond. She liked to think of Tim there, watching over them. Still loving them.

She still missed him, and she knew that Will did, too.

In that way, she guessed, she did have a guarantee. *Love is eternal. It's the only thing that lasts.*

"Is she out there?" Will asked, bringing Gretchen back to reality.

She looked over at him. The cold had made his cheeks glow, and deepened the blue of his eyes.

"Do you think? In the depths?" Will turned to face her, and Gretchen realized he was talking about Asia, not Circe.

"Somewhere," Gretchen replied. Asia had disappeared two days after that night, and they had not seen her since.

"She was never comfortable around us. Humans, I mean," Will explained.

"I can imagine that."

"She was even ready to kill me. And she thought of me as a brother."

Gretchen squeezed Will's hand. "She would have killed me, too. And she was right."

Will's eyes met hers, and she felt their connection like a touch. "You couldn't have killed anyone."

"No."

He leaned toward her, pressing his warm lips against hers. It was a soft kiss, lingering and full of love and restrained passion. Will twined his fingers through Gretchen's long hair, and a thrill ran through her.

"Oh, God, get a hotel!" Angus shouted.

Something cold and wet showered over her, and Gretchen realized that Mafer had just tossed a snowball at Will.

She let out a shout as Will jumped from his seat to grab a handful of snow. In a few moments, a full-scale snowball fight was on. Even Gretchen joined in.

It was all so easy, so carefree, she couldn't resist it.

Just like normal life.